# *Dragons of Draegonia*

## *The Adventure Begins*

## *Book 1*

by

Michael W Libra

Grosvenor House
Publishing Limited

This book is published by
Grosvenor House Publishing Ltd
28-30 High Street, Guildford, Surrey, GU1 3EL.
www.grosvenorhousepublishing.co.uk



A CIP record for this book
is available from the British Library

ISBN 978-1-908596-77-2

*Dragons of Draegonia is dedicated to my four grandchildren, George, Grace, Joel and Zach who listened in awe when very young and growing up into their teens, still wanted to hear more.*

*Michael W Libra*

*My thanks go to Ronnie Gunn for his time taken in the editing, Katerina Danailova for her excellent illustrations and my wife Ann for her endless patience and contribution.*

# Prologue

The Dragons of Draegonia is a tale of fantasy and make believe. It has humour, intrigue, adventure and suspense. Written specifically for children, the story line nonetheless, should make many adults smile, if their imaginations have not been warped with age.

The volcanic Island of Draegonia was first inhabited in the early 5$^{th}$ Century when dragons fled from across all areas of the world from a growing population of humans' intent on their destruction. The uncharted island was first located in the middle of the Pacific Ocean. Unfortunately, as time passed, explorers from Spain, France, Portugal and England came very close to discovering the island, placing the dragons once again, at immense risk. The Island originally had some 400 dragons roaming its lush green land but to-day, only half of these have survived.

To maintain their secrecy, a 'Wizard Dragon', cast a spell that made the Island invisible and have the magical property to disappear and reappear in different locations of the World's Oceans and Seas at will. A further spell of the 'Wizard Dragon' created a time anomaly. Seasons and time became stretched compared to that of human time. Fifty days on Draegonia would only be realised as one human day spent.

But no human being had ever visited the Island, until now..........

# Chapters

## Chapter 1

# The Island of Draegonia

In an ocean, far, far away, lies an island that no human being has ever set foot upon. It is an island that appears and disappears at will, fading into a sea of mist when ships or aeroplanes come within radar or viewing distance. This strange and mysterious island is the Island of Draegonia.

It is a magical island that changes its location at will, never appearing in the same spot twice and never revealing itself to any other islands or land.

The island is shaped like a large squashed witch's hat, not quite round and very lumpy in the middle with a stumpy top. The centre of the highest peak conceals the almost perfect round smoky mouth of an active volcano. The highest point of the island, known as Volcano Peak, holds dark secrets, secrets surrounding the disappearance of more than 170 dragons.

The island has two very distinct and differing coastal formations. The bottom part of the island known as South Side, is flatter, with golden sands dashed with small glistening particles of coral that stretch from the lapping water's edge up a slight gradient to the edge of a tropical forest of tall palm trees, the trunks of which are hidden in part by thick lush foliage of dark and light green shrubs and bushes. In summer these bushes are covered with flowers and blossom of pinks, reds, oranges and yellows and are home to a plethora of insects, numerous birds and small animals.

Travelling from the south northwards, towards the centre of Draegonia, the trees and shrubs become thicker still, entangled with sweeping intertwining vines that look like thick ropes of a spider's web. The canopy of the palm trees blocking out much of the sunlight and with little air movement, generates enormous heat, resulting in an atmosphere that is shadowy, humid and very eerie.

If you were to move further and higher inland, most of the trees become smaller, thinner, being replaced by thicker more prickly shrubs littering the sides of several steep rough tracks, bordered by large rocks and boulders. These tracks become more rugged and steeper still as they circle the uppermost and more mountainous sector of the island.

It is in this part of the island that the tracks lead to pathways that narrow further, opening onto ledges with steep drops, some difficult to access, others impassable and most hidden from would be visiting eyes.

Although the centre of the island appears jagged, climbs skywards and looks inhospitable, there is hidden from obvious view, accessed from only two points, a large flatter ledge secluded beneath the towering, weirdly shaped, smoky and very old volcano. Here lies the City of Draegonia.

The volcano itself definitely has a life of its own. Sometimes, when bathed in sunshine, it is quiet and docile. It can be seen raising its giant head towards the pale blue skies, making wheezing noises as it puffs out rings of bluish white smoke, just as if it were snoring in its sleep.

But at other times, especially when the weather is bleak and the seas become violent, throwing up huge amounts of cascading water all around the island, the volcano grumbles, bellowing out huge amounts of thick greyish black smoke from its cavernous round mouth, propelling tongues of red and white flames, high into the stormy skies.

On the western side of the volcano, two deep indentations reflect powerful yellow, blue and red flames, as though the volcano has two very scary, bloodshot eyes. The volcano violently vibrates when it becomes angry, shifting boulders from its sides with protruding angular rocks that look like large muscular arms.

Close to the bottom of the volcano, beneath numerous, smaller, and narrower ledges, there is a labyrinth of many passages. Some lead to Draegonia Central, the homes of the islands sole inhabitants, the dragons!

Dragons have lived on the Island of Draegonia for well over 15 centuries. Most are friendly but all fear the wrath of one particularly evil and most frightening dragon of all times, **Dragon Black.**

## Chapter 2

# The Dragons of Draegonia

Dragon Black, like all the other dragons of Draegonia, is named after the colour of his skin. His skin is thick with a smooth armour plated scaly surface. Like his temperament it is very dark, in fact it is jet black. All dragons fear him and have had to accept him as the unelected King of Draegonia and their one and only leader.

Dragon Black rules with an iron claw, sets the rules, passes the laws and makes all the decisions.

Black is both fierce and very bad tempered. He is always in a bad mood and especially dislikes anyone disturbing him. His presence is felt even when he cannot be seen. He breathes out vast volumes of fire from his nostrils and as he moves his huge, now very overweight, body from side to side, his large black claw feet, drive massive foot prints into the ground, sending shock waves all around him. Dragon Black's fearsome looks and size and awesome fire power has guaranteed a life of luxury, being waited on by all around him.

Dragon Black was once the only dragon that could fly - an attribute he had engineered - but because he has put on so much weight, Dragon Black is now grounded. However, his wings when fully extended make him look a most frightening and fearsome creature. Dragon Black spends most of his days sitting on the magisterial throne situated in the Great Hall. He presides over the Council of Dragons, snarling out orders, thrashing his long tail to confirm his authority.

Dragon Black is lazy, fearsome, a bully and very dangerous. Those who dare to contest his authority seem to just disappear, never, to be seen again.

Not all of the dragons are like Dragon Black. There are two sister dragons, Dragon White and Dragon Cream. They always have a smile and usually never get angry. Dragon White and Dragon Cream have very important jobs. They are the lookout team and beach cleaners of Draegonia. Dragon White patrols the beach to the south of the island and Dragon Cream, who is a little heavier, (She also eats far too much) patrols the bleakest and rockiest top part of the island called North Island. Here the seas often cascade with thunderous noise, shooting sprays of angry white foam into the air. The sandy beaches were replaced long ago by the cooled down molten lava spewed out over decades of activity from the island's volcano.

Of course Black, White and Cream are not the only dragons on the island. There is Dragon Green, a most jealous dragon who envies all others. He believes he should have had the job of patrolling the beaches that Dragon White and Cream have. He also wants to be Mayor, he wants recognition. Dragon Green always wants what others have and never does anything helpful. Green is not trusted by many of the other dragons, especially Dragon Brown.

Then there is Dragon Pink, the youngest of all dragons. She is very pretty and petit and glides around the Island of Draegonia smiling at everyone and everything. She loves playing with the animals in the wooded areas. In fact Dragon Pink is the only dragon that appears far friendlier and less frightening. That's why her best friends are the small animals of Draegonia who rarely venture too close to the other dragons, but love to play with her.

Dragon Pink is also comical to look at. She wears a shiny silver skirt that has many layers of soft tissue, material that puffs up when she spins round, very similar to that worn by a ballerina. The animals love to watch her dance and join in with her as she sways to music created by the wind blowing through the rustling leaves of bushes and trees, accompanied every so often by the sound of cascading waves.

Two other dragons, who also live on Draegonia, close to the centre of the town, are Dragon Red and Dragon Blue. These two are employed by the Mayor of Draegonia, Dragon Gold, who has always suspected Dragon Black of evil crimes, but is in constant fear of him.

Dragon Red is in charge of the Fire Service. Not putting fires out but starting them. You see, when dragons get ill or have a cold, it is possible for their flames to die. This is called 'Flame Out' and that's when Dragon Red of the Fire Starting Brigade (FSB) comes to the rescue. His amazing flames have never gone out and his role is to breathe new life into those dragons that may have dying flames, requiring what is called, reheat. Dragons who are unable to regain their flames eventually die, thus a dragon's inability to spit flame is life threatening. Flame Outs, however, rarely occur and thus Dragon Red is not kept busy. In fact he has not been called upon for Dragon Centuries. Although very important himself, Dragon Red looks up to the wise and peace keeping Dragon Blue.

Dragon Blue is, of course, head of Draegonia's Police Force and it his job to keep law and order. This is made quite easy, as no one would dare to do anything to upset Dragon Black, so Dragon Blue has little to do, other than sleep in his cavern that overlooks most of the township of Draegonia, supported by two part-time dragon officers.

Other dragons living within Draegonia include the identical twin Lilac Dragons who are in charge of refuse disposal, Dragon Brown a senior officer of Draegonia's Army, Dragon Yellow who seems always to disappear when things become frightening and Dragon Grey who is the island's doctor as well as personal physician to Dragon Black.

There are of course many other dragons each varying in colour matching their mood, character, occupation or disposition, but more on these later.

Apart from the animals, the volcano and of course the dragons, no one else lives on Draegonia or has ever visited, that is until one day when the sea and sky met together to see who was the stronger, resulting in an almighty argument and violent fight, that created one of the worst storms in living memory.

## Chapter 3

# The Adventure Begins

The storm had been brewing for many days as the sea and sky continually met in great anger to discuss who was more powerful. The argument raged, with the sea throwing up most of the contents from its sea bed high into the sky. Crabs, octopuses, whales, shells, bits of ship wrecks and rocks all fired into the sky as the mighty sea swelled up, rolling a series of cascading waves some 70 feet high.

The sky equally responded by hurling lightning bolts, shooting hailstones down from high and together with his friend the wind, caused a gale, the like of which had never been seen before. The wind roared, the thunder clapped, as the sky drew its shutters together blocking out the rays of the ever fading sun. The ocean was soon plunged into a frightening darkness, broken intermittently with flashes of blinding illumination from forked lightening, every high voltage flash highlighting, in sharp black and white contrast, the surf breaking to the tune of thunderous roars.

In amongst this frenzy of rough seas, high winds and pouring rain with sky and sea arguing as to who should own what, a small timber laid craft that looked like a smaller version of a pirate ship, could be seen battling to stay upright.

On board the little sailing boat 'Princess' battling the elements, were four children, Joel, George, Zach and Grace.

The four could not believe they were fighting to save their little boat from overturning. None could believe they were in the middle of an ocean and certainly could not understand how they found themselves all together, in a storm of such ferocity.

The last thing they recalled, was boarding their little craft for a trip down the river. They could remember that their parents had said to be careful and not go too far. Yet here they were, out of sight of land, soaking wet, cold and very frightened.

George the eldest, he was twelve and a bit, told the others to be brave and not to worry. "I'll get us out of this just hold on" he commanded as he lowered the sail to storm position. "Don't be scared Grace" he shouted again.

Grace, a few months younger than her cousin looked up at George from the safety of the cabin and held tightly onto the hands of her two younger

brothers Joel and Zach. “I want to go home” shouted Zach. “I want Mum and Dad” Joel cried out. Grace knew she had to be brave, being older than her two brothers. “Hang on to me; don’t be scared, we will get through this.” She said reassuringly above the chaos and ear splitting noise, although not quite believing it herself.

A huge wave cascaded across the floundering boat, sweeping George off his feet, over the side and into the violent foaming sea. He had attached to his belt earlier, a safety line securing him to the wooden side rail of the boat, but this had inexplicably snapped and swept overboard, he was swimming for his life.

Grace, seeing George disappear into the black and white foaming sea, rushed for the life belt hung on a rail close to the steering wheel. She pulled at it with all her might and as the boat once more propelled itself up a huge wave, managed to lift the life belt off its hook. She quickly threw it over the side, in the direction where she last saw and thought she could hear George, yelling for help.

Joel and Zach, both hearing the commotion, rushed out of the cabin, each grabbing Grace by one hand, their other hand’s clinging on to her waist in fear she too, would be washed overboard. What was she to do? There was no one at the wheel and she certainly could not steer the boat, even in normal waters.

Earlier the engine had stopped because they had run out of fuel, so 'Princess' was now at the mercy of the pounding seas, being thrown in all directions.

Her first thoughts were for survival. She quickly checked the life vests of her brothers and then tightening her own round her waist she headed for the life raft. On the front of the boat was a small white round container that had a red band round it. This was the life raft and Grace knew that if she could get to it and pull the emergency handle it would open forming a life raft with a canopy. Once inside she, Joel and Zach would be safe.

Then, Grace felt her hands go limp. She realised that the boys no longer were holding onto her! They were gone!

The boat, now at the top of a huge wave was starting to crash down the other side. Spray was coming from all directions and Grace could not see a thing. Then, she felt a tug on her sleeve. It was Joel, he had started to crawl towards the life raft with Zach when he heard a loud cracking noise. Was that another burst of thunder? Was it a gun shot? No sooner had these thoughts rushed through his mind, when he saw the small boat's mast break mid way and topple towards the steering wheel where Grace was still standing. Zach jumped up and ran past Joel and stretching out his hand, he too tugged at Grace's other hand in an attempt to protect her. Both boys each holding with one hand onto bits of the boat to steady themselves, tugged and tugged at Grace, finally pulling her away before the mast came crashing down. Grace had no time to think or indeed thank her brothers, as the tiny boat now was in between two more very large waves that were about to engulf them.

With Grace out of danger, Zach took the initiative and headed back to release the ropes holding the life raft container to the bow of the boat. Grace and Joel fought their way back, with Grace shouting to the boys to hold on to her, as she pulled the emergency release handle.

Several things seemed to happen all at once. A loud bang was heard as the gas-filled arming device expanded the life raft in seconds to its full size. The little boat swung first to the right then seemed to point skywards as the seas once more erupted. The toppled mast swung back, pushing the life raft towards the edge of the boat. If action was not taken soon all would be lost. Two huge flashes of lightening followed in swift succession suddenly turning night into day. The little boat finally decided to give up its fruitless battle and began to sink stern first. Just as Grace thought that all was lost she heard a familiar and welcoming voice.

George had not realised how important a life vest was, until now. He had been thrown in all directions, tossed around by the enormous waves each trying to drown him. But, every time one wave pushed him under the frothing sea foam, his bright yellow sea jacket popped him back up. But he knew it would not keep him afloat for long in seas that were becoming more violent by the second.

Then it happened. A large round red and white safety ring, with the name 'Princess' in black lettering, hit him on the head. He let out two yells. The first was because the ring was quite heavy and it hurt, the second, a yell of relief, because the life ring would keep him afloat. Two more flashes of lightening and a large thunderous noise - George looked into the blackness, broken only by the greyish white spray of thousands of gallons of water cascading from all directions, to see the little boat 'Princess' coming towards him.

He yelled, but it was of little use. The storm, crashing seas and howling winds were no match for his little voice. Another loud crack and this time he saw the mast break in half and fall towards the rear of the boat, the broken spar suspended by a solitary rope. He knew that his cousins were in deep trouble. As the little boat rushed past him, George suddenly let go of the life ring. He had seen dangling from the little boat a trailing line that was tethered to its stern. George realised this was another safety line similar to the one he had been tied to before his had sheared. With an almighty heave he yanked at the rope managing to grab hold of one of the fenders that still remained dangling over the side like a swollen sausage. As he hauled himself once more on board he could see that Grace had armed the life raft was crouching down with her brothers, he let out a yell.

"Quickly," he shouted, "the boat is sinking, get in the raft and I will join you." Grace relieved and pleased to hear George's voice pushed her brothers towards the raft's welcoming entrance. Joel was first to get in followed by Grace. George had noticed that Zach had grabbed hold of a large bag and was struggling to lift it as the breaking waves were making it heavier. George lifted the bag and grabbing Zach pushed both into the open hole of the raft. There was another flash of lightening making visible the three worried looks as George joined his cousins, telling them to hold on to each other.

How they managed to get inside the raft pulling the canopy entrance tightly shut behind them was lucky, as the boat was now being violently tossed around, but what followed was miraculous. A huge wave picked up the raft and its contents of children, sweeping it high into the air and moments later crashing it down into the black swirling sea. The little boat was swamped, keeled over and finally disappeared.

For what seemed like years the life raft was thrown up and down and from side to side. The four children did not say anything but just held very tightly on to each other and even though it was noisy, cold, wet and very rough, one by one they all fell asleep in each other's arms.

On the Island of Draegonia Dragon Blue was on patrol at the highest point of the island looking out to sea, admiring the storm that was subsiding. He liked the noise and thought the thunder and lightening seen earlier was great. Also on duty working the northern beach picking up stranded fish and throwing them back into the ocean cauldron was Dragon Cream. Both dragons were peering into the storm and both dragons saw what they thought was a brightly coloured pimple appearing on the blackness of the sea. Dragon Blue exclaimed to himself, "Umh, the sea is starting to break out in spots." Meanwhile however, Dragon Cream could see that this particular spot was moving around and getting nearer and nearer to the north side of the island.

She ran up and down keeping her eye on the red and yellow rubber life raft that now could be clearly seen. Then all of a sudden, it disappeared from view. The raft was grabbed by a swirling tidal current taking it down towards the southern side of the island. Dragon Cream made a few more runs up and down the beach and then slightly exhausted gave up. Dragon Blue who saw the pimple disappear from his view went back to the police station to enjoy the most important leisure time activity of sleeping as the sun lifted itself out of the sea making the sky slightly friendlier. With that, the ocean also decided to take a rest. Calmness was being restored, but Draegonia was about to receive four visitors that would change the lives of the dragons of Draegonia for evermore.

## CHAPTER 4

# All Washed Up

George woke up with a start. What was that noise? George had been asleep cuddled up with his cousins Grace and Joel with Zach sprawled across their feet. It had been a terrible storm and even though the noise had been frightening George and his best pals had managed, mainly through exhaustion, to fall asleep. The problem now was that all of them were wet and cold caused by the waves pounding on the little rubber life raft, making the reddish orange canopy to leak in several places. Drips of water were still plopping onto his head when he heard that noise again. **Whoosh** it went. It sounded like one of mum's sighs when George had been somewhat naughty, but a great deal louder. **Whoosh**, there it was again. Grace opened her eyes and seeing George peering out of the opening of the canopy, she whispered. "What's that George, where is the noise coming from?" George motioned his hand indicating that Grace was to remain quiet, something that she often found very difficult to do. "George" she shouted, her loud screech wakening Joel and Zach, who jumping up with a start, moved either side of George putting their heads also out of the canopy.

The three boys could not believe their eyes. Their little life raft had now washed itself up on the golden sandy beach on the south side of Draegonia and there, a couple of hundred metres to their right and in the middle of the sandy beach, was an enormous white dragon. **Whoosh** it went, spitting out another enormous flame from its huge mouth. The two boys, either side of George, looked at each other and quickly removed their heads from the canopy opening, snatching it shut behind them. Joel looked at Grace and said. "Sis you're not going to believe this but we have just seen a huge white dragon blowing fire from its mouth." "Oh you two, you're always joking, I don't believe a word of it." With that, Grace crawled over to where George was kneeling and with one swift movement of her hand, fully opened up the canopy and jumped out of the raft.

Dragon White had thought it was about time for her breakfast. She had been up most of the night due to the noise of the storm and was clearing the beach of all drift wood that had been washed up. **Whoosh,** another flame propelled from her mouth, **Whoosh, Whoosh** two more huge flames sprang twenty feet across the beach setting fire and devouring all the drift wood and other rubbish washed up in its path. Then, she stopped. What on earth was that? She spied, at the water's edge, a round strange object. It had a peculiar orange coloured head with a mouth that strangely opened up to reveal a pair of eyes. Then there were three pairs of eyes, then one pair, or was it two? Almost immediately the mouth opened right up and out popped a very strange creature. Dragon White had never seen anything quite like it before and considered her options. She could ignore it, she could run or she could attack it with the hope it would be frightened off. Dragon White decided to attack.

Grace stood motionless by the water's edge unable to believe her eyes. She looked straight across at a large white dragon, who obviously was thinking about its next move. The white dragon peered back at Grace, its quizzical eyes glinting in the early morning sunshine. For a split second neither moved. Then all of a sudden the tranquillity of the early morning stillness was broken, as an ear piercing scream came from Grace. A scream that not only frightened all the birds perched high up in the trees that on mass shot high into the sky squawking and screeching their warning cries, but a scream that also for a split second sent a shiver down the long white tail of Dragon White.

White's jaw opened in dismay, she puffed and a red and white flame shot high into the air. Dragon White was uncertain and slightly afraid but knew she had to do something. Was the noise from this animal a call to alert others, or was it a form of communication? Dragon White started to move towards Grace. She had decided attack was her only option.

Grace, on seeing the dragon start to move towards her ran from the water's edge, up the beach, towards the cover of shrubs and trees. Dragon White, with increasing speed followed, her head bowed low, snorting as she rushed towards Grace, puffing out streaks of fire with every sand-splattering bound.

Grace did not look back, but dived headlong into the shrubs and rolling over peered out between two very thick bushes. The dragon had lost sight of her but Grace could feel its hot breath on her face as Dragon White nosed the bushes that concealed her.

George, Joel and Zach had not fully understood why Grace had charged out of the raft but could see an enormous white dragon chasing her. As Grace disappeared from view into the shrubbery the dragon caught up and was now pushing with its huge head the shrubs and bushes from side to side, snorting as it did so.

The two oldest boys, leaving Zach behind, jumped out of the raft and sped up towards the white dragon shouting and waving their hands. "Pick on someone your own size!" shouted George, "Leave her alone!" cried Joel.

The dragon, hearing the yells of the two boys turned and with a mighty thrash of her tail clipped them both with one sweep, tossing them high in to the air. **Splat, Plop,** both boys flew through the air landing on their backsides. Fortunately their fall was broken by landing and bouncing off the rubber life raft. Picking themselves up they scrambled inside and joined Zach.

The dragon, determining that two animals cornered in a raft was better than one hidden in a bush, stomped down towards the water's edge and the reddish orange craft.

George, seeing the dragon approaching knew that they were in imminent danger, picked up the first aid and survival kit that is kept in all life rafts and found what looked like a large hand gun. The cartridges for this flare gun were clipped together in a pack of four. These were also inside the yellow plastic bag that carried the gun and emergency locator radio. Each cartridge, the size and shape of a cardboard tube found inside toilet rolls, was divided into two sections. The base of the cartridge held the powder that when ignited by the gun's firing mechanism propelled it towards its target, whilst the top part, coloured red, housed the explosive charge and magnesium. Magnesium is a powder that when ignited burns and makes a powerful white hot flare that can be seen for miles. The cartridge now placed in the gun made it a very useful defence weapon.

George pointed the loaded gun at the approaching dragon, took aim and squeezed the trigger. There was a loud BANG, the bullet or what George was soon to discover was an explosive flare, was propelled from the gun at great speed, aiming straight for the dragon. The dragon, taken completely by surprise, stopped dead in her tracks, opened her mouth in amazement and precisely at the same time swallowed the incoming ballistic missile.

There was an explosion followed by a lightening flash of light giving off tremendous white heat. The dragon's mouth suddenly became very, very hot and without any help from her, huge red, blue, yellow and white flames shot out high into the sky. So strong was the flash of light caused by the explosive charge in the dragon's mouth that she became for a few moments, blinded. Unable to see, Dragon White stumbled on the sand and toppled over rolling down the slight gradient towards the waters edge. Still unable to see, her whole body turned, her large front legs splayed out in front of her and head between them like an arrow, headed for the sea. White's mouth was still very wide open with bursts of angry flames shooting out uncontrollably in all directions with her every outburst of growls and moans until she came in contact with a enormous wave and swallowing several gallons of sea water and several clumps of floating grotesque looking seaweed, she totally extinguished her flames. There was nothing left of her dragon fire but small rings of black smoke drifting either side of two, very bright red and furious eyes.

George and Joel took their opportunity, ran frantically towards where Grace was hiding and with giant leaps jumped over the first few shrubs, landing close to a crouching Grace, who had her hands firmly clasped over her eyes.

## Chapter 5

# Wanted

Dragon White, up to her knees in salty water, something dragons care little for, slowly picked herself up and staggered to the waters edge. With a very large shake of her body she rid herself of thousands of water droplets, making a small rain storm. The sun glinting on the droplets made a number of mini rainbows appear, each displaying colours of blues, yellows, greens and reds. Dragon White opened her mouth and growled but other than a roar and a couple of confused looking fish popping out, no flames appeared, **her fire had fully extinguished,** she had **'Flamed Out'.**

White again made a mighty roar, this time sending a shivering vibration through the air at the annoyance of losing her ability to spit flames. Although Dragon White was usually quite a placid dragon, when aroused or annoyed she could be quite frightening. And right now, Dragon White was most annoyed.

Who, and more particularly, what had caused this catastrophe? Dragon White knew she had to report the entire incident. There were strangers on the island, they had removed her flame and were obviously a danger to all other dragons. Stomping off, White made her way round the edge of the lush grass, bushes and trees, taking the longest but easiest trek, back to the centre of the island and safety.

In the centre of the city, the streets of Draegonia were quiet apart from the grumpy noises of Dragon Black. Even the volcano was asleep with faint plumes of white smoke curling from its huge mouth in time with little rumbles that sounded like snoring. Dragon White, slightly out of breath and still trying unsuccessfully to breath out fire, ran breathlessly to Dragon Blue's residence.

A large sign could be seen showing that Dragon White was now outside the premises of Draegonia Police Station. Inside, Dragon Blue was fast asleep making odd grunts and snoring sounds. Dragon White rang the bell. No movement was heard, so White rang it again.

Dragon Blue lifted his head and in his most assertive tone bellowed "Just a moment and I will be with you." Blue got up and as he passed a full length mirror made out of highly reflective steel, obtained decades earlier from shipwrecked vessels, he gave a once all over look at himself and realising that this was obviously an official call, put on his dark blue waistcoat and tightly fitting police cap and opened the door to his office. There, silhouetted in the bright sunlight was a very out of breath Dragon White.

She looked even paler than ever. "Come in, and what can I do for you?" Chief Constable Dragon Blue demanded, as he laid down a flat rock for her to crouch on. Dragon Blue also crouched down on his haunches behind his official desk. His solid stone desk was covered in very important looking tablets of stone, pieces of paper like material and what looked like 'Dragon Leg Chains'.

The construction of Draegonia Police Headquarters was similar to most of the other caves of Draegonia. It was hewn out of the side of the volcanic mountain. But inside, the similarity ended. It was much larger and had many corridors, some leading to individual cells others to living quarters. Dragon White entered the largest and main room of the station trying to compose herself. The walls were covered in blue and white stripes and every so often, hanging on big hooks, were pictures carved in stone of dragons wanted for questioning. The pictures were very old for on Draegonia no one dared to break the law as Dragon Black had a particularly nasty way of dealing with offenders.

It was said that in olden times when all dragons could fly that criminals were taken up to the top of the volcano and thrown into the mouth to be consumed by flames. White shuddered at the thought and explained to Chief Constable Blue that she had been clearing the beach of driftwood when she was attacked by some very strange creatures. "They arrived on the island in a very peculiar craft," she said. Dragon White further reported to Dragon Blue that she had fought for her life and that after a great struggle the attackers had run off but not until they had stolen her ability to roar fire and spit flame.

Blue listened intently and took lots of notes engraving them with a pen like instrument held in his claws onto very smooth flat stones, so thin they looked like thick parchment. "This is very serious," he said. "We must inform Mayor Dragon Gold and also let Dragon Black know that we have been invaded."

Dragon White lowered her head, had she made too much of the incident? Had she told all the truth? Had she exaggerated a little too much? As she was thinking of perhaps telling Chief Constable Blue that it was in fact only four small creatures and what really happened. Dragon Blue pressed a large red and white button marked EMERGENCY. The noise was immediate and deafening. Loud clangs of a bell could be heard throughout the island and the large flashing blue light close to the top of the volcano started to pulsate, flashing on and off alerting all on Draegonia that a serious incident had occurred.

Dragon Red had been looking forward to another quiet day as he was painting his office a bright red. In fact he had painted everything red. Red floors, red door, red windows, and red ceilings. The only problem of course, was that when he was in his cave he could not be seen, because he too was red all over. Hearing the alarm bell he looked out of his freshly painted bright red window up towards the top of the volcano and the flashing blue light. Dragon Red dropped his brush and can of paint splattering his shiny black 'Fire-dragon Boots'.

He knew something major was up, as the emergency alarm to his knowledge had never been pressed before. He jumped into his Red Fire truck and sped quickly round to Chief Constable Blue. As he arrived, he could see Dragon Blue was gluing a reward notice onto the blue information board situated outside the main entrance to the Police Station.

In large blue letters on a white background the notice informed.

*WANTED 500 DRAEGONIAS REWARD FOR THE CAPTURE OF DANGEROUS FIRE STEALING INVADERS*

Seeing Dragon Red approaching after alighting from his fire tank, Dragon Blue put down his glue bucket and brush and explained to Fire Officer Red what had happened and specifically that Dragon

White had lost her flame. Dragon Red trotted across to where White was standing and asked her to open wide. He examined Dragon White's mouth thoroughly asking her to cough and spit some fire. No matter how hard Dragon White tried, she just could not raise a spark let alone a flame. Dragon Red knowingly shook his head, this was the first time he had to re-flame any dragon, but he knew what he had to do. He removed from his tank a white can with the words 'Highly Flammable' in red, painted on it.

"Stand back" he said as he poured the special fluid into White's gaping mouth. "Stand well back" he said again and aimed from his mouth into White's own mouth a fine narrow beam of very hot flame. Dragon White felt a warm sensation as the heat penetrated the back of her throat. There was a flash and her flame ignited. She roared with relief. "It's back" she exclaimed, but her euphoria was short lived as her flame became smaller and smaller until with a little puff of smoke, it went completely out.

Dragon Red scratched his head. **"Ummn"** he declared, "not enough 'Dragon Fuel' I think." He poured the remainder of the fuel into White's mouth, drenching the residue of the flare fired earlier by George and the bad smelling seaweed she had swallowed. "This will do it." Dragon Red took a long deep breath and aimed another flame towards

White's gaping mouth. Tears came to White's eyes as Dragon Red's flame was unleashed. This time it was far hotter and more concentrated. What happened next took everyone by surprise. From White's mouth there exploded a huge ball of fire followed by thick black smoke that enveloped her and everyone else. As the smelly sticky black smoke cleared White could be seen with large tears in her deep bluc eyes. She sneezed with thousands of droplets of the sticky black stuff spattering Dragons Blue and Red. White's black smudged face carried a frown. It was now very clear that her flame had not come back. A flameless dragon - what was she going to do? She had totally 'Flamed Out'. This was very serious.

Chief Constable Blue and Dagon Red huddled together in quick conference. "Right" Officer Blue said "I will report this to the Council of Dragons, Dragon Red, you take Dragon White to Draegonia Hospital." Dragon Red opened the roof of the fire truck in order that White could sit upright. She still had black smoke and sticky stuff pouring from her mouth and was violently sneezing; the last thing Dragon Red wanted was for the inside of his bright red fire truck to become contaminated with dirty black droplets splattering everything with each thunderous sneeze.

As they drove off, Dragon Blue took some large keys from under his tiny wing like arms and locked the cave entrance, then charged off for a very important emergency meeting, with the Council of Dragons.

## CHAPTER 6

# Survival

Grace, George and Joel had watched as the very large white dragon had shaken every droplet of sea water off of its now very dirty greyish white skin. Dragon White had gathered herself together and had disappeared out of sight towards an opening where the beach and tightly packed shrubs and trees met. All three breathed a sigh of relief. It had been a very frightening experience.

"That was close" said Joel. "I thought it was going to eat us" said Grace. George said nothing. "So what do we do now?" Grace wanted to know, looking to her friend and hero George. "I am not sure but one thing we need to do is to get away from here before that dragon and its friends return" George confidently replied. He knew that someone had to take charge and as he was the eldest it was up to him. "Come on stay close and follow me." As the dragon had slinked off following the edge of the beach where the shrubs adjoined and disappeared into a narrow clearing, George decided that they should perhaps go inland and as far away from it as possible. He knew that the trees would provide shelter and give them some opportunity to hide. "One moment George" Grace shouted with some authority. "We should take with us all the supplies from the life raft. I am sure they will be needed." Joel had taken this as his job and before his sister had delegated the task had started to run back towards the beached raft.

Zach had been hiding inside the raft and was wondering where the others had got to. He had heard the commotion of the dragon, had felt the shock waves hitting the life raft as the dragon had slid into the sea and from his vantage point saw the dragon limp off into the distance. Now in front of him was his brother Joel.

Zach grabbed the bag that held food, dry clothes, some water bottles and a yellow packet of safety and survival equipment, while Joel put the rest of the life raft's odds and ends, plus emergency radio, into an orange canvas bag that had two thick straps so that it could be worn as a back pack.

"Come on Zach" Joel commanded picking up the bag and struggling with what appeared to be the heaviest items. Turning back towards where George and Grace were standing, Joel urged Zach to be quick.

Zach knew that the tide would be coming in and that if they were not to lose the raft it would be necessary to pull it further up the beach. He was strong for his age but could not budge it. By now it was half full of water and was rubbing along the soft waters edge, making it very difficult to shift. "Here let me give you a hand." It was Joel. Seeing Zach struggling had placed the bag back into the raft and was yanking at the rope tied to its front. Both young lads heaved and strained and with great effort managed to drag the raft all the way up to the top of the beach and into the undergrowth.

"What are you two doing?" Grace demanded. "We haven't got time to play with life rafts, why didn't you just leave it on the beach?"

Both boys smiled with Zach letting out an enormous sigh. "Phew, if we had left it where it was it would have been washed out to sea and we just may need it to get off this place." Joel nodded in support and covered the raft with some fallen palm leaves.

Grace grabbed the orange back pack and with her nose in the air stormed off. The three boys continued to smile at each other, each taking an item from the raft and made after her, for they knew that once Grace had decided that she was going to be the leader, it would be far simpler for all to follow her.

The sun was now high in the sky with its rays protruding through the gaps of the rich leafy

canopy of the trees. "Did you hear that George?" Grace said "It sounded like an alarm bell." George and Joel both heard the muffled yet distinctive sound but did not say a word. Zach cocked his head to one side. "I think it's coming from up there," he said pointing to the tip of the glowing volcano that could clearly be seen in the distance. What was now on their minds was where exactly did the noise come from, what was making it and was the pulsating beat made by friend or foe?

The ground started to get steeper and rougher in parts, with the odd boulder protruding from the foliage. The trees were thinning out and it was getting hotter as they moved further inland. The four very hot children stopped for a rest sitting on one of the larger rocks and taking water bottles from Zach's bag, each had a well earned drink. "Don't drink too much," George said, "at least not until we find more water." Grace nodded but continued to drink. Joel put his bottle in his pocket whilst Zach sipped the last droplet. "You'll be sorry Zach," said George, "especially if we cannot find any more!" Zach just grinned, for he knew that his brother Joel had plenty and he could always share with him. Joel almost knew what Zach was thinking and patted his bottle to make sure it was safe.

In the distance they could see the top of the volcano and what appeared to be a blue flashing light. Joel, peering into the distance, said very thoughtfully,

"I wonder what the sound of all that clanging and that flashing light means?" Grace said nothing. She was just finishing off the last drops from her water bottle. "I am not sure," George replied, "but we have nothing to lose by going towards it. At least it shows there is some form of life there."

"Well let's hope they know how to deal with dragons" Grace retorted, as she gathered herself together and once again, taking the lead, conducted the trio of boys further towards the centre of Draegonia and closer to the lair of dragons, who were holding an emergency meeting in the prestigious central cave. This contained the all-important Great Hall of the Draegonia Dragons.

## Chapter 7

# The Council of Dragons

The Great Hall of Draegonia was the most important meeting place in Draegonia. Housed in the very centre of the largest group of caves it represented the authority of Draegonia, passing and implementing all laws. The vast meeting hall had several openings, many hidden in the dimly lit corners with corridors leading to other caverns. It was said that one such exit led to a secret tunnel where Black disposed of those who he considered a threat, but this had never been sighted or proved to exist. The Great Hall contained the seat of power, a throne made of solid gold raised on a platform of dark grey granite where Dragon Black was now crouched.

He presided over the ruling Council of Dragons, each identified by different coloured sashes laid diagonally across their chests. The sashes designated the seniority and position of each dragon, although seniority and position counted little when dealing with Dragon Black.

Dragon Blue was now joined by Dragon Red and both were immediately surrounded by several other dragons who were thrashing their tails snorting out fire and generally arguing amongst themselves. "A complete search of the island is called for." "Yes I agree," several of the dragons were overheard to mutter, as they gestured their approval.

Amongst the cacophony of sound, Dragon Black slowly eased himself up from his golden throne. As he did so he brushed his head on one of the silver-grey stone arches that supported the high carved out rock ceilings. Black's body curved forward, his eyes piercing all beneath him in the dimly lit cavernous hall. Black looked angry and formidable and it was clear to all that he was not in a good mood. His eyes glinted fiery red, his large mouth opened displaying scores of sharply pointed teeth each with razor-saw like edges. Blasts of yellow and red flames shot out of his mouth, grey plumes of smoke snorted from his nostrils. He growled, "These intruders are to be found and dealt with. We cannot have trespassers on our island, especially ones who are so dangerous that they are able to extinguish our flames." A murmur of agreement came from a group of dragons encircling Dragon Black. "Who is going to deal with them?" The Mayor Dragon Gold demanded, "We have no real army, just our small in numbers, dragon police force." All eyes turned towards Dragon Blue who, embarrassed by the attention, coughed and was just about to respond when he realised that his flame too, was getting smaller and smaller. Not wishing to draw any more attention to himself he raised his head and with his paw like claw just covering his mouth coughed and in an authoritative voice informed the gathering that he had no doubt that the trespassers would be arrested and charged within the next 48 'Dragon Hours'.

The dragons stamped their feet and pounded their huge paws together in thunderous applause. Smoke and flames bellowed out of their nostrils and mouths, their heads swaying from side to side. The gathering of dragons looked awesome, and the heat from their flames and thickening smoke from their nostrils made for a most frightening scene.

Amongst the clatter of self congratulations, one softly spoken but quizzical voice could just be made out. The dragons ignored the question - "How?" The question again was raised by Dragon Brown, an old warrior, who was one of the oldest and wisest of dragons on Draegonia. "HOW?" Dragon Brown demanded, but this time raising his voice for all to hear.

The hullabaloo of growls and snorts died as both Dragons Black and Gold spun round and glared at Dragon Brown. "What do you mean HOW?" demanded Dragon Black. "Well," Brown continued, "firstly, HOW are you going to find the invaders? Secondly HOW will you capture them and thirdly HOW are you going to protect us from invaders that seem to have weapons that can snuff out our fires?"

The Council of Dragons looked at each other, some scratching their heads, others rolling their eyes and all looking rather stupid. "YES, HOW are you going to apprehend these culprits Dragon Blue?" demanded Mayor Dragon Gold.

Dragon Blue sank back on his haunches, looked at all the dragons that were all staring hard at him and thought for a moment. "I really don't know" he exclaimed "we have never been invaded...." Before Dragon Blue could finish, a confident loud voice was clearly heard above the all the snorts and sighs.

"We must first gain as much intelligence about them as possible, what they are doing here, how many of them there are and what are their weaknesses?" The statement came from Dragon Brown who had now moved towards Dragon Black. "Sir" Brown continued, "many years ago, before I came to Draegonia as a tiny dragon, my father was known as the bravest and fiercest dragon of a place called Britannia. The gathering of Dragons became silent as Brown continued with his story. "Unfortunately my father was badly wounded by a dragon slayer called *Saint George a knight of the realm, but before my father died, he carried me to this island of Draegonia and during our journey, taught me all his secrets of battle and one important lesson in particular, to know all about your enemy." The dragons peered at Dragon Brown in awe and amazement and started to chatter amongst themselves. Dragon Brown was well liked and respected and although recognised as a soldier, few dragons had seen him as a leader and none had thought of him as a defender of Draegonia. In fact, none of the dragons had dared to assume any position of authority not bestowed on them by Dragon Black, in fear, that he would take it as a threat to his own power.

Dragon Black had ruled Draegonia under an umbrella of fear. It was rumoured that those who

---

*The most famous legend of Saint George is of him slaying a dragon. In the Middle Ages the dragon was commonly used to represent the Devil. The slaying of the dragon by St George was first credited to him in the twelfth century, long after his death. It is therefore likely that the many stories connected with St George's name are fictitious.
There are many versions of story of St George slaying the dragon, but most agree on the following:

1. A town was terrorised by a dragon.
2. A young princess was offered to the dragon
3. When George heard about this he rode into the village
4. George slew the dragon and rescued the princess

had contested his leadership had mysteriously disappeared. Black was also directly responsible for the fact that the dragons could no longer fly, as at their fifth Dragon Birthday, all dragons had their wings clipped. The law was introduced by Dragon Black so long ago that only the eldest of dragons could remember the days they could fly. Now, as they had all lost the power to fly they were stuck on the Island of Draegonia and unfortunately stuck with Dragon Black.

Dragon Black stared hard at Dragon Brown who he had thought for some time might cause him trouble. Black was disturbed that the council were now giving perhaps too much reverence to him.

Black thumped the floor with his giant tail bringing the uncontrolled chatter to an abrupt halt. Looking straight at Brown he said. ***"We will appoint you as Commander in Chief,"*** Black growled. ***"You will take Dragons Red and Blue to assist you. Also, have Dragons White and Cream search Draegonia for these trespassers and you may appoint any other dragon necessary to end this assault on us."*** Black paused for a moment, then placing his head close to Brown's he said menacingly, ***"Make sure you do not fail, because if you do!!!"***

All the dragons gasped, looked at each other and anxiously towards Dragon Brown, as a tremendous vibration ran through the floors and walls of the hall, as Black thumped the ground three times with his mighty tail, signifying that the meeting was over and that **he** had made **his** decision.

As the final thump of Black's tail resonated throughout the chamber, there was one dragon, hiding in the shadows, with a sly smirk on his bright green face.

He was Dragon Green, a dragon that was not that well liked as he always wanted what others had. He was known to be a jealous dragon envious of everyone. His bright green scaled skin now glowed in the gloom of where he was hiding. He had heard of Brown's appointment to Commander in Chief. Why had **he** not been chosen? Why was **he,** not asked for **his** help?

Green was now extremely envious of Brown's appointment; his green skin was getting brighter and brighter by the minute as he became uncontrollably jealous. Green had made up his mind that he was going to show them all that the Council of Dragons had made a big mistake in entrusting their safety to Dragon Brown.

Slinking further back into the shadows, Green began formulating a plan that would make him the hero and Brown an incompetent fool. But first, he had to be the one to bring important news to Dragon Black and the Council of Dragons. Green needed to be seen as the saviour of Draegonia, this was his golden opportunity. Devious thoughts rushed through his wicked brain. Grabbing a flaming torch affixed to the rocky wall, he headed for a side exit and into a dimly lit corridor that climbed up towards the lookout post. This had the advantage of visibly covering all the southern part of the island.

Dragon Green, was about to make a name for himself.

## Chapter 8

# Green with Envy and Black with Spots

It had been quite a trek for the four shipwrecked children. Grace was still charging ahead closely followed by the three boys as they made their way deeper inland towards the centre of the island. "Come on we need to get there before night fall."

"Get where?" George asked. "There silly" Grace declared as she pointed her hand towards the smouldering volcano. Joel kicked a smooth round stone as all four stopped and stared. The stone rolled a few feet before gaining speed as it disappeared down the rough but very steep ground.

They had been walking for hours and the terrain was becoming increasingly difficult to cover. They had now left the shade of the tall trees well behind them with the lush green grass and shrubbery having been replaced with short stubby clumps of dark green leafed bushes interspersed with patches of tall course brownish thin stems of wild grass. Moving even further inland, both sides of the track were punctuated every so often by larger rocks and boulders endorsing what was becoming an inhospitable scrubland, supporting numerous taller dense brown bushes with protruding prickly stems. As they climbed higher still and closer to the lair of Draegonia's Dragons, they paused nearby to some tall jagged rocks; the lengthening shadows making it feel much cooler, as the four passed beneath them.

"I need a rest" Joel wheezed. He was out of breath. He had been carrying the large bag from the life raft that had been repacked and now contained ropes, first aid pack, water (what little was left), matches, several tea bags, a packet of dried milk, VHF Radio and the gun with the remaining unused cartridges that earlier had saved them from what appeared to be an attacking white dragon.

"O.K, let's make camp here while we still have sufficient light to see what we're doing" George said sympathetically, seeing that his pal Joel was completely exhausted. "Where will we camp?" shouted Zach who had been lagging behind. "Over there" Grace pointed towards three very large rocks. Two of them formed a V shape; the third rock was flatter and overhung the tops of the other two, providing a natural safe shelter, with views of the darkening sea reflecting the brilliant orange and pinks of the early evening sky.

The sun, shaped like a large fire ball casting long narrow shadows of all who stood within its dying rays, was moving closer and closer towards the horizon, sinking slowly into the sea. The gentle breeze that had kept them cool during the heat of the day had suddenly become quite cold.

George shouted as he ran towards some small thinning green and brown shrubs close to the large inverted rocks spotted by Grace. "I'll collect some wood for a fire if you prepare some food for us Grace, come on Zach, give me a hand."

The two boys searched for firewood as Grace and Joel prepared a makeshift camp for the night, using the boulders as protective walls and the overhanging rock as shelter. Although there were numerous bushes and shrubs around, their pencil-thin stems were only useful to start a fire. To keep a fire burning required thicker wood and after some time of searching George and Zach returned with an assorted mix of twigs and thicker gnarled dead wood ideal for a small fire just sufficient to boil some water to make a welcomed hot drink.

"Is that all you managed to find?" moaned Joel, who was tired, cold, very hungry and becoming quite irritable. Grace opened up one of the individual survival packages containing some food that obviously by the state of its faded and torn packaging, had been in the life raft for some time. "UGH," she had bitten into the hard biscuit and taken a piece into her mouth. "This is horrible" she exclaimed indignantly. “If you think I am going to eat this you have another think coming.” “I’ll eat it” Joel cried out grabbing the round disk like object. He bit hard into the biscuit and swallowed. “Typical” Grace exclaimed, “you’ll eat anything.” The four children sat round the fire eating, drinking the freshly made tea and discussing how they were going to get off the island and of course how they were going to hide from any more dragons.

Whilst they chatted, the deep red ball of the sun finally sank majestically into the rich rippling blackness of the sea. As it did so, shadows produced by the ebbing fire danced around the rocks and with the crackling of the last of the flames the fire dwindled into no more than hot ashes. “Is there any more fuel for the fire?” Grace quietly asked. “No afraid not and anyway it is getting quite late” George replied, “the best thing we can do right now, is rest and sleep; nothing to do until morning and it would be dangerous to try to walk in the dark.”

Joel and Zach had already opened up the blankets taken from the backpack and were placing them neatly on the ground inside the safety of the sheltered rocks. “I am still hungry,” Joel moaned. Zach put his hand into his pocket and pulled out a very small bar of chocolate he had found in the bottom of the survival bag. “Here take this” he whispered, but don’t tell the others.” Zach, although the youngest of the group, believed he was tougher than his elder brother Joel and that he had to protect him. “Thanks Zach” Joel said, taking the chocolate bar and downing it in one go, “you’re a real pal.” Zach just gave a cheeky grin, for he knew it was true.

With the beds laid round the dying fire all four snuggled against each other for warmth and one by one drifted into the land of dreams.

The cold breeze of the night air swirled round the sleeping children. The now, not so hot ashes, blown by the cool evening breeze sparkled, creating a mass of little red and yellow glows. Some were lifted high into the blackness of the night sky, their flashes of tiny lights like hundreds of small flaming torches, mixing with the silver pin pricks of light, from a million stars.

Dragon Green had reached one of the viewing platforms and was surveying the southern part of the island. He had been contemplating what he was going to do. He wanted to be liked, he wanted to be respected, and in fact he wanted to be like Dragons Blue and Gold whom he envied because of their power and seniority. He craved respect and authority. He thought how great he would be as the Mayor of Draegonia. All these thoughts took time to pass across his mind. Some might say it was because his head was so large it took time for any thought to travel across it.

Green knew it would be almost impossible to have Blue or Gold's position but now was working out a devious if not dangerous plan.

Green had decided that he was going to make Dragon Brown's task of catching the trespassers difficult. He was also going to feed Dragon Brown with misinformation to make him look foolish. Green chatted to himself (no one else would normally listen to him) working out a way for him to be seen as a major player in the defending of Draegonia. Green had visions of dragons patting him on the back and thanking him for being so brave that they would promote him to Brown's role of Commander in Chief and that everyone would be bowing in his presence.

Green stared into the night sky, smiling as he had visions of being made a hero. What was that? Dragon Green had caught sight of hundreds of small lights moving around. He strained his eyes peering into the blackness of the southern sky. "Obviously the invading army," he mumbled under his breath. "There are so many invaders that Dragons Brown, Blue, Red and the two sisters White and Cream will never be able to deal with them, at least not without my help." He continued to talk to himself. What Green did not realise of course, was that these flickering pin pricks of light were not from the torches of an approaching army of dragon beating warriors, but just the last sparkling embers of four youngsters' fire, being wafted by the breeze into the cool night sky.

Green rushed off to find Dragon Brown who, outside the Dragon Police Station, was in conference with Dragons Red, Blue, Grey and the two Sisters, White and Cream.

Dragon White had been released from Draegonia Hospital as they could do no more for her. She was still coughing and spluttering with black droplets continually being sprayed over everyone as she sneezed and sneezed repeatedly. Dragon Blue was unhappy, explaining that he too was now unable to spit any flame from his mouth. "Me too" said Dragon Red. "What?" exclaimed Brown? "Yes Sir," said Dragon Red, "my flame has also gone out, what is happening?" The dragons were so engrossed in conversation that they did not see Dragon Green approaching. "Hey" Green shouted as he scampered up. "They're coming and by the number of lights I saw there must be a whole army of them." He hurriedly continued: "the invaders are heading this way from the south and will be here very soon unless you do something fast."

Dragon Brown spun round to see Green standing right in front of him. "How do you know?" Brown demanded, "I thought as Dragon White was unwell that I would patrol the southern side of the island," Green continued with his exaggerations, lies and false claims. “I could see the lights of their camp in the distance, there must be hundreds of them, and I expect them to be warriors’ intent on taking over Draegonia.”

Dragon White took a long deep breath, she was just about to explain that earlier all she had seen were three very small two legged creatures and a funny looking orangey container that may have had another hiding inside, all washed up on the beach, when she started to violently sneeze again. She sneezed and she sneezed - in fact she couldn’t stop sneezing and with each loud explosive sneeze, torrents of black droplets flew in all directions.

On hearing the commotion dragon heads appeared from all the surrounding cave entrances and windows, each quickly pulling back as they were splattered with numerous black sticky droplets. “For goodness sake use a ‘Dragon Hanky’ or put your foot up to your mouth,” cried Dragon Cream, who now looked more like a ‘Dalmatian Dragon Dog’. Green wiped his chest looking at the black bits on his pointed claws. “Well, what are you going to do about all this, Dragon Brown?” Green demanded.

Dragon Brown was of course very concerned, not just at being informed that Draegonia was in the process of being invaded by a much larger army than had been previously thought, but that other dragons were also losing their ability to spit flame. Was there a connection? Was this a secret weapon they had? What WAS he going to do?

Brown thought for a brief moment before he addressed his so-called troops who had not fully realised they were now conscripted into Draegonia's Armed Forces. "I think we had better set up dragon defences around the base of the volcano to protect the city. Dragon Cream you should go with Dragon Green to where he has located the invaders' camp in order that we may have precise figures as to how many there are. In the meantime Dragon Red and Dragon Blue you both need to have a medical check up to see what's causing your Flame Outs." Brown continued giving commands: "Let me have the station keys Dragon Blue, Dragon White you notify the Mayor to issue a 'Dragon State of Emergency', we must get everyone to the Great Hall where I shall inform them of the battle plans."

Dragon Green smiled. He knew that Brown was going to make a big fool of himself as surely he would not be able to deal with what Green thought was such a large invading army. "I think you need all the help you can get Dragon Brown, so why don't I check out the invaders' camp site and bring back the information to you? Let Dragon Cream patrol the northern part of the island, just in case the invaders decide to attack from there as well." Dragon Brown thought for a moment, and then said

"Good idea Green. Dragon Cream, off you go and both of you" Brown paused looked at his dragon pocket watch then bellowed, "**and** report back to me any relevant information!" Green and Cream saluted (it seemed the right thing to do) and trotted off in opposite directions. Dragons Red and Blue with Dragon Grey leading scampered off to the hospital for their examination, leaving Dragon White, still coughing, to run off to alert the Mayor and everyone else that they would all be required to attend the Great Hall.

Dragon Brown was left on his own. It was getting late and the moon was casting its eerie glow over what was now a deserted and much quieter street. He opened up the police station cave door marched across the cavernous room and pressed the Red and White button causing for the second time that day the alarm bell to clang and once more illuminate the flashing blue light. Brown closed the door, locking it after him and with thumping strides marched briskly off to the Great Hall.

Dragon Green had trotted well out of sight of the police station realising that he had volunteered to put his own life at risk by spying on the invaders. He crouched down on the hard ground and thought for a moment. Thinking aloud he said, "I know, I will pretend to have spied on the invaders' camp site. There must be at least a hundred of them and obviously as some of us are losing the ability to spit fire, the invaders must have a weapon that we do not know about. I'll pretend to have seen it." Green had confidently decided, that whatever the strength of the invading army, they would be no match for Dragon Black.

Green finalised his story and rehearsed it to himself a few times as he headed for the Great Hall. At last he would be respected and considered brave and important. His reported observations of the threat would prepare everyone, they would win the battle and he would be a hero. He gave a wry smile as he thought of the medals he might receive for his bravery.

Inside the Great Hall Dragon Brown was discussing the feared imminent attack with Dragon Black as scores of other dragons flooded into the chamber to join those who were members of the Dragon Council. Some had their night caps still on as they had been rudely awakened by a coughing dragon. Some were comparing notes about their 'Flame Outs' while others just arrived with worried and frightened looks.

The meeting was roared to order by Dragon Black. He growled ***"We believe that there is an invasion of our island, Dragon Brown has reported that he has been advised that hundreds of troops have been sighted and are going to attack us and that at least three of our dragons have already lost their flames and that this may well be connected."***

The congregation of dragons burst into grunts and groans as the importance of the meeting made its impact. Some were roaring at the top of their voices, their failing flames spitting in all directions. There were other dragons who were displaying the tell tale black spots of a sneezing dragon. Their flames also appeared to be getting smaller and smaller.

Before Dragon Black could raise another growl, Dragon Green rushed in. He had a bandage around his head with stains of what looked like blood. In fact it was 'Tomato Dragon Sauce' that he had applied for effect a few minutes earlier. The Council of Dragons rushed to his assistance. "It was horrible" Green panted, "they jumped me but after a struggle I managed to get away!" All eyes were on Green as he explained that he had gone to spy on the invaders' camp but before he could see how many there were several had seen and attacked him. Dragon Brown put an arm round Green, telling him that he was a brave dragon and asked him if his injuries were severe. "How did they cause the head injury Dragon Green?" asked Brown. Green slightly taken by surprise and not having thought about how he might have got the injury responded in a fraught voice: "They clubbed me, hit me over the head." Gasps were heard from the dragons listening intently to Green's encounter with the enemy. "Four or five maybe more I couldn't tell, it was so dark, they just pounced on me" Green hastily continued, "they hit me with large club-like things."

"*Describe these warriors?*" Black barked. "Yes," interrupted Brown, "how tall were they? What did they look like? How did you escape them and did they follow you here?" Dragon Green fought for words but clearly he was not prepared for all these questions, instead he decided to keel over and pretended to feint from his pretend injuries. Thump, his body hit the floor. Dragons rushed from all directions to his aid. Some brought water and one was heard to offer to give him the 'Dragon Kiss of Life'.

Dragon Green, on hearing this, quickly opened his eyes and staggered to his feet assisted by several very supportive dragons. "He is a hero." "Jolly good show." "He should be given a medal." Dragon Green felt a sense of pride, he was being recognised as a hero, his plan was indeed, working.

*"What are those black spots?"* Dragon Black asked Dragon Brown, pointing to Green and to all the other dragons who carried the dreaded black sticky spots that Dragon White had coughed, spluttered and sneezed all over them.

At that precise moment Dragon White, exhausted from her messenger duties appeared. Rushing into the hall she blasted out yet again, an enormous sneeze, this time splattering and fully covering Dragon Black with the same droplets that marked every dragon on the Island of Draegonia, which is every dragon, bar one.

## Chapter 9

# In the Pink

Dragon Pink also had heard the alarm for the second time that day and she could see once again the flashing blue light situated high on the volcano, silhouetted against the late night sky. Pink, earlier that evening, had gone for a walk to practice her dance routine she was too embarrassed to do in front of other dragons. She was the youngest and smallest of all the dragons. She had very soft pink skin, a small tail and trim body. Her dragon head was also small and roundish with two bright blue eyes either side of a squat snout that displayed a very cute smile. Dragon Pink did not frighten anyone or anything. This was just as well for as she danced in the moonlight she moved closer and closer towards some very large rocks where four children were fast asleep.

George woke up rubbing his left leg that had pins and needles in it. He had been sleeping quite heavily when he was awoken by two noises. The first was a clang, clang of a bell in the distance, the second a noise of something moving close by in the blackness.

"Wake up" he said pulling at Grace and prodding Joel. "Do you hear that?" he whispered. "Hear what?" Zach said loudly, rubbing his eyes. "Shush!" Grace responded putting her hand over Zach's mouth. "What is it?" she whispered. "I don't know but it is getting closer" George replied searching in the bag that lay beneath Joel's feet. George's hand grabbed a torch and with one movement he pointed and switched it on, its fine bright spot light swept left and right. Joel and Zach followed the beam with their eyes straining into the darkness to see what had made the noise. Grace stood behind them clutching the flare gun used earlier that day against Dragon White. All four children remained very quiet hardly breathing, waiting for what they believed were fierce dragons about to attack them.

Dragon Pink was just finishing the last of her triple pirouettes; her tiny feet thudding on the hard ground when out of nowhere shone a brilliant white light encircling her and her performance. Somewhat surprised she stopped her interpretation of 'Dragon Swan Lake' and stared into the light. Her two little eyes became smaller, reacting to the light as it passed her by. The bright beam paused then came back and shot off into the opposite direction. It stopped again and this time slowly came back to where she was crouching. What was this thing? Pink became quite worried and started to stand up on her back legs to peer into the direction where the light had come from.

George could not believe his eyes. Grace started to laugh. Joel crouched in amazement mouth open, unable to say anything and Zach rubbed his eyes in disbelief. "Shush Grace" George said quietly. "Is that a dragon?" Grace enquired, still trying to suppress another giggle. "I think so" George replied. "But what's it doing wearing a ballet skirt and is that a tiara on its head?" cried Grace. Joel had now closed his mouth and also started to laugh followed by Zach, Grace and George. All four were laughing so much that they had not realised the dragon was now walking slowly towards them.

Dragon Pink could not understand what was making the light appear. Whatever it was it made peculiar noises and it was coming from where there were some large rocks. Dragon Pink slowly walked across to where the four intrepid explorers were in fits of laughter pointing at Dragon Pink. In between the laughs Dragon Pink could make out voices and to her amazement understood what was being said. Tears started to appear in Dragon Pinks eyes as she realised that these little things were making fun of her. They seemed to be pointing to her tiara and skirt and making unkind remarks. Dragon Pink sat down right in front of the children and with a shake of the head rid herself of her tears, and in a quiet low pitch voice said "It is not nice to make fun of dragons." The children abruptly stopped laughing.

"Did you speak?" Grace asked, looking at the dragon. "Yes, it is not nice to make fun of me, I am very upset, I do have feelings you know." George looked at the dragon rubbed his eyes and pinched himself. No, he was not dreaming, yet this dragon had actually spoken to them. "Wow!" Joel exclaimed "a talking dragon, wait until I tell them about **this** at school." Zach moved closer to the dragon and pinched her soft pink scaly skin. "It's real" he exclaimed. "Ouch" Pink cried. "Who are you? What are you?"

Grace felt sorry for laughing and apologised profusely. "Leave it alone Zach" she commanded. Joel nodded in agreement as George went closer and with a nervous finger prodded the dragon to also make sure it was real. "That's George, I am Grace and these are my brothers Joel and Zach," Grace said in a cool clear crisp voice. "We are from a place called England. Our parents let us go sailing but we got caught in a very bad storm, our boat sank and we ended up here."

George seeing that there was no imminent danger from this strange night visitor offered it a drink pouring the last of their water into a large plastic bag retrieved from the survival box. The pink dragon with one lick took all the water and smiled. Her smile was warm and gentle and the four immediately knew they were in no danger.

Joel shivered, "Please don't be frightened," the pink dragon said. Joel responded indignantly, "I'm not,

I am just very cold." The embers of the fire that had helped to keep the children warm had long gone out. The dragon could see that these four funny looking little things were friendly but in the blackness of night were indeed cold. Dragon Pink recommended that they find some smooth round rocks and place them where the fire had been. Before Grace could question why, the two lads started carrying several stones that had been close to the entrance of their new camp. Grace looked on thinking that everyone had lost their minds. George placed the last stone on the pile that now completely covered the old fire and asked. "What are we doing this for?" Pink did not answer instead she took a deep breath and fired a red hot blast towards the stones. Her flames grew brighter and brighter creating a deep blue and purple glow. Within seconds the pile of stones so carefully placed by the two boys, first glowed red, and then white hot, giving off tremendous heat. The three children sat round the glowing stones and beckoned the dragon to join them. Dragon Pink trotted forward and sat down to a barrage of questions.

Grace wanted to know where the dragon lived, did she have a family. George was interested to learn where they were, and could she help them get off the island. Joel's tummy rumbled as he asked where they might get some food.

Dragon Pink was great company; she explained that the noise and the flashing blue light that they had seen would have been set off by the 'Dragon Police'. She told the children about Draegonia and all about Dragon Black, the Council of Dragons and how none of the dragons, except Dragon Black could fly. "Why can't the other dragons fly?" Joel asked. Dragon Pink, embarrassed, shuffled her front paws and flicked two tiny wings that had been hidden until now from her sides. Because Pink was so young, her wings were intact, but too small to assist her to fly. The children watched as she started to flap each little wing in turn. Dragon Pink went on to explain that when dragons reach a certain age their wings are clipped at the root to prevent them from flying.

"That's terrible" cried Grace." "But why?" piped up George who was tidying up the makeshift shelter to provide room for all of them to sleep. Dragon Pink's eyes glazed over as she bowed her head forward so as not to let anyone else other than the children hear what she was about to say. "Dragon Black does not want any of us to leave. He has all the Dragons of Draegonia looking after him, we are no more than his slaves."

Dragon Pink moved to where George had cleared a space, laid down and rolled on her side with one large front paw holding her head, her elbow making a small indentation in the hard ground. She continued but in a slightly quieter and more frightened tone of voice. "Dragon Black passed a law that all dragons were to lose the ability to fly" she continued, "and his rules are not to be challenged, for those who do, they just disappear, never to be seen again." Dragon Pink gave a massive yawn, placed her head upon the floor, closed her eyes and just before falling asleep whispered "I only wish he could be replaced with someone kinder."

"Come on you two" George moved alongside Dragon Pink where his blanket lay and settled down for what was left of the night. "We have a big day tomorrow, it is very late, let's all get some sleep." Joel and Grace responded by cuddling up together, whilst Zach moved closer to his super pal, George. By the warmth of the dragon heated rocks they all fell into a deep sleep.

## Chapter 10

# Lies and more lies

Dragon Brown had adjourned to a side chamber of the Main Hall with a number of dragons following at his heels. Although suspicious of Green's interpretation of events and what appeared to be such a gigantic injury that would have laid any other dragon out for weeks, Brown decided to give him the benefit of doubt. "Green, I need you to monitor the invading army and its progress so that we can ensure our defences are in place. I recommend that you take Dragon Yellow and you both get as close to their camp and report back to me their every movements." Dragon Yellow had tried to remain inconspicuous as he was a real coward and was surprised at being conscripted into Brown's newly formed army.

Yellow's body shivered in fear, "I'm afraid I can't assist" Yellow snorted, "I have a bad cold, my flame is very, very weak and almost nonexistent, got spots developing all over me **and** I have a bad back." Dragon Brown ignored Yellow's excuses. "You always have a bad back and a cold so what's new, and we all have problems with our flames, that's why every dragon has to do their duty, and there will be no exceptions." Yellow's jaw dropped open in dismay, he usually got out of anything that was dangerous or even mildly challenging, but here was Dragon Brown, who seemed to be in total command, ordering him into what he thought to be imminent death.

Dragon Green was studying the unfolding events intently. What was he to do? He surely could not have any dragon too close to him, especially now when things were going so well and definitely not anywhere near him while he was conjuring up more imaginative stories. But then he had a 'Dragon Brainwave'.

Yellow was really a big coward, he would not want to go anywhere near any enemy or any dangerous situation and if given the opportunity would hide or take the easy way out.

Green decided to take charge of the situation. "Come on Dragon Yellow, we'll keep out of sight and at a safe distance and just observe and study the invaders." Green's little brain was working overtime. "I'll get the closest to the enemy's camp and report things back to you so that you in turn can take the information back to Dragon Brown. You'll be a sort of special messenger."

Green had made his mind up that Yellow would be no threat to his aim of being the only hero of the day. And Dragon Yellow, he was relieved to know he would be at a safe distance from any danger. Brown, with another deep frown appearing across the top of his forehead, scrutinised both dragons and in a commanding voice barked. "So what are you waiting for? GO!" And with the command resonating in both dragons' ears, they were just about to scurry away when they both spied Dragon Gold in the distance.

Brown, for a brief moment thought as to how and why Dragon Green had changed, why was he being so helpful and agreeable? But Brown's thoughts were immediately interrupted by Dragon Gold's noisy clanging chain of office bouncing from side to side as he ran into the chamber with great urgency. "We have a horrendous problem now" he gasped. "The hospital has reported that all dragons carrying the black spot plague have lost their ability to shoot flames and that every dragon on Draegonia has now become infected."

Gold continued in a hurried and fearful voice "Dragon Black has decided that the invaders are probably using chemical warfare and that their leaders must be taken alive in order that we can obtain an antidote from them." There was a mumbling from several on-looking dragons, each carrying the black spots and all having trouble to spit flame and fire.

Brown listened intently to Dragon Gold, his eyes narrowing, his furrowed brow deepening further as he had two major challenges facing him. The first was to identify who, out of the recently reported hundreds of invaders, their leaders may be and secondly what type of antidote would they have and how was he to obtain it.

Gold continued, "Also, Dragon Black wants you to put Dragon Green in charge of capturing their commander in chief," Gold paused, "that's if they have one."

Dragon Green preened himself. He was to be put in charge. And before any dragon, especially Dragon Brown, could raise an objection, Green pushed Dragon Yellow through the chamber exit. On exiting into the street Green issued an order to Dragon Yellow to follow him. They headed at great speed to where Dragon Green earlier had seen flashes of tiny white and the occasional reddish sparkling lights. After what seemed ages, both dragons came within 'Dragon Seconds' of where four children and a pink dragon were still all curled up and fast asleep.

Yellow grabbed Green's arm and both dragons came to an abrupt stop. "Look you were attacked," Yellow puffed, "and only just managed to get away, what good will it do for both of us to get captured or worse?"

Green was hanging on to every word spoken by Yellow, for he was also concerned but for different reasons. He had lied about being attacked and as with all lies it required more lies to continue such fabrication. What was he going to do? Another plan formed in Green's brain: he would leave Yellow and go on ahead to reconnoitre, he would then come back and provide information for Yellow to take back. If anything went wrong he would say that Yellow had misinformed or made it up to get out of actually fighting the invaders. Yellow, he knew, was a coward at heart and would be only too pleased to wait in safety and let him take the decisions and all the risk.

"OK, Yellow, you stay here, I'll obtain the intelligence for you to return it to The Council of Dragons and you can take all the credit, as I am already considered a hero," Green slyly pontificated. Without any further chat, Green trotted off towards the area where he had earlier that night had seen the sparkling lights, leaving Dragon Yellow mopping his sweating brow and breathing a huge sigh of relief.

Whilst all this was going on Dragon Pink had stirred from her sleep. She could see the first few rays of the early morning sun painting the black sky with shades of orange. Not wishing to awaken the four children, she slid quietly away from their rocky enclosure. So silent was she that Dragon Green never heard or saw her but, as he crept silently over the brow of the ridge separating the children's camp site from the two dragons, he spied four unusual beings curled up and asleep around a pile of now, not so hot, rocks.

What were they? Were these part of the invading army that he had reported and where were the rest of them? Green shuddered. Was this all, had he made a huge mistake? He crept nearer for a closer look and as he did so caught his foot in a crevice that hurled him head over heels sprawling on the hard ground and with a massive thump came to rest behind some very tall thick bushes. Four startled children jumped up. One screamed, one shouted, one yelled and the other, George, waving his arms furiously, picking up a stick, hurtled some 20 meters towards where Green was nursing some bruises.

Green saw George and the other creatures racing towards him and assumed this was the beginning of a fearsome attack. He immediately jumped up, did a one hundred and eighty degree full turn in mid air and hurtled back in the direction from which he had come. The four children stopped in their tracks looking on in amazement and as the green dragon disappeared from view, chattered vigorously, interrupting each other, about what they had just seen.

What had become of the pink dragon, had it been a dream? No it couldn't have as they had all just seen a green acrobatic dragon, jump from the ground, do a mid-air turn and then disappear from view. What was this island and why were there so many dragons of different colours? And how many more would they come across? The three stragglers (they just could not keep up with George) were now in deep conversation. Joel, interjecting that he was hungry and wanting his food, Zach intent in fighting off any more intruding dragons, Grace raising question after question without waiting for an answer, was soon rejoined by an out of breath George, who quickly restored some order.

In the distance, and out of sight of the four, two dragons, Yellow and Green, collided with each other. Just as Yellow had thought he was safe and preparing to settle down for Green's return, a fleeing Dragon Green looking more over his shoulder than where he was going, ran straight into him.

"Quick," Dragon Green yelled, "Get back to Dragon Brown tell him that **we** have four of the invaders cornered and that after a short battle, WE have frightened the army into retreat and as we speak now, they are leaving the island!" Green had decided that he had made a grave error in making everyone believe there were hundreds of troops but on seeing the size of the four (unbeknown to him) children, he could imagine that such an army of little people would have run, on seeing two dragons such as Yellow and him. Yellow picked himself up, looked at Green in disbelief and said," What do you mean **we?**" "Well" responded Green, "do you want to have everyone believe you did nothing but sit on your haunches whilst I fought them off on my own, do you want everyone to think" Green paused and with a faint smile continued, "that you were a coward and did not try to help? **Or** would you like to take some of the credit and inform the Council of Dragons and Dragon Brown of our heroism and your part in cornering the invaders' command centre?"

Yellow did not want his true yellow colour to reflect his image or reputation; he wanted to be brave but never quite managed to be. Yes, he would run with the message and he would take any glory that Green was so magnificently sharing. "Right, I'm off and will get assistance, how many will it take to bring back the four and are they the ones in charge?" Green thought for a brief moment then again with a rye smile said. "Tell them we have, no you have immobilised them and that they have no fight left in them. Inform Dragon Brown we should only need Dragons White and Physician Grey and on your return with them, the four of us will round up the invading generals and bring them in." Yellow started with some haste to run back to the centre and turning slightly, shouted over his shoulder "But what did I do to assist you?" Green's answer was short and to the point, "You did everything to chase the army off the island, just make it up." Yellow was running so fast that he did not realise he was being unfortunately set up and that very soon he would be made to look very foolish.

Dragons Brown, Blue, Red, and Gold, were seated in the Great Hall with Dragon Black, the all night session showing on their tired faces. They were discussing in detail with Dragons Grey and White their verbal reports. Dragon White still wanted to explain about earlier, when she had seen the little craft and the tiny people and the fact that she definitely had not seen an invading force, when Dragon Yellow hurtled in.

"We have fought and frightened the invaders off" Yellow yelled. "They are taking to the sea in small crafts" he further exaggerated. All the dragons turned their heads towards Yellow. "And as they were so small and no match for the two of us I and Dragon Green chased them off, with their tails between their legs." Yellow was so full of the importance of his role, he forgot that earlier, Green had carried a bloodied bandage and wounds of a battle, with what he now was confirming as a fearful force.

Dragon Black only reacted to the fact that the invaders had been repelled and with a very rare smile on his face congratulated Dragon Yellow for his and Green's remarkable bravery. Yellow was the centre of attention, something he was not used to, and as such continued with the story he had rehearsed on his way to The Council. “It was my role to chase off the invaders as Dragon Green had cornered the army’s generals” he continued with his lies. “We have them a couple of ‘Dragon Miles’ away in the scrub land hiding behind the rocks, pleading for mercy.”

Yellow loved the adoration and admiration coming from all around him but one of the dragons was not entirely impressed. Dragon Brown interrupted Yellow’s flow and said, somewhat quizzically. “So Dragon Yellow, how many were there in the army you chased away? What weapons did they have? How did you manage to repel them without any fire flame? And more to the point, why did their generals stay behind, only to be captured?” Yellow was now a little stuck for words. He had not reckoned on being questioned in so much detail, so he had to think very quickly on his feet, something he had never been used to.

“Well,” he slowly started, “the main army I could only see in the distance, they had obviously decided to leave the island thinking that perhaps a smaller force would suffice.”

“So why did they leave four generals behind with such a small force and what is the strength of this remaining army? And, will the others, who you say,

YOU chased, be back with the main force?" Brown cross examined. Yellow was floundering it was obvious that Brown had severe reservations about the whole saga.

"Brown, you're reading too much into what obviously is a very brave action from two of our finest and heroic dragons" Dragon Black bellowed. "Yellow, where is Dragon Green right now?" "Well Sir," Yellow said puffing out his chest at being referred to as heroic, "Dragon Green has the invading generals cornered a couple of 'Dragon Miles' away and we can bring them in for questioning with the assistance of Dragons White and Grey, well that's what Dragon Green suggested."

"Good idea," agreed Dragon Black. "The three of you should bring them in immediately for questioning and confiscate any weapons they may have." Black continued, "Dragon Blue and Brown go and organise the interrogation rooms and arrange four containment areas so that there is a cell for each of them."

Brown, turning from a hard stare at Yellow's twitching cheeks spoke to Dragon Black. "Dragon Blue can arrange the cells, I'll go with them Sir to assist and verify the intelligence."

Black snorted, "Totally unnecessary, Dragon's Green and Yellow appear to have everything well under control, no real thanks to you and your efforts are obviously not required by them. You go with Dragon Blue and prepare the cells, Gold and Red you stay with me, the rest of you **MOVE.**"

Outside the Council of Dragons Main Hall, numerous dragons could be seen running in all directions, some scampering off with the news to others and many preparing themselves for the imminent arrival of the prisoners.

## Chapter 11

# The Capture

Green taking as much cover as possible afforded by the thick shrubs had been crawling back and getting closer and closer towards the four intrepid travellers. His steely devious eyes were now watching their every movement. He was considering, why were they not armed? How small they looked and what were they doing on the island?

George, out of earshot of the other two boys was quietly talking with Grace. George pointed towards the island's centre. "You know we should be very careful as we get closer to that volcano. We have seen three dragons now, White, Green and Pink and I am sure there must be more!" Grace nodded her head in agreement and diverting her eyes towards Joel and Zach, she said. " I think Joel should keep close to me and you take care of Zach" she continued more in a whisper, "if we get separated let's meet back at the life raft and hope someone will find us soon." George was in agreement and with a reassuring smile added. "You know I am not too sure that those dragons are more scared of us than we should be of them. Think about it. The white one was not particularly scary especially when it did the submarine impersonation, the pink one was kind of sweet and that green one looked as though it was frightened out of its life by our shouts and screams." Grace thought for a moment. "Look" she said "let's try to find the pink dragon and ask it to help us."

"OK guys" George beckoned to the lads, "Collect everything and let's go."

Zach and Joel picked up the survival bag and Grace and George gathered all other items, checking to make sure nothing was left behind. The fire had long gone out and the rocks heated by Dragon Pink were now stone cold, but Joel kicked dust and gravel, more as a safety precaution to prevent any of the dry brush from catching alight.

Dragon Green watched as the morning sun rays added warmth to the hard ground. From his almost flat, crouched position and on all fours, he was studying their every move. Was this a war dance? He saw Joel kicking the ground and Zach running in circles as he picked up various items ready for their departure. Dragon Green was crawling nearer thinking of his next move when all of a sudden George spotted him.

Green tried to hide, by burying his head in a clump of taller bushes, but with limited cover and his back side now sticking way up in the air, as he crawled towards the four, he was easily visible to all. Green looked very stupid, especially from George's point of view.

"Hey" shouted George moving towards the dragon, "Can you help us?" The green dragon dropped his mouth, his eyes bulging. "Are you talking to me?" he asked. "Yes" said George as he approached somewhat cautiously, "Why did you frighten us earlier and then run off, we need help?"

Green raised his head and haunches, stretched to his full height and with a broad sickly grin moved closer towards George. Here was Green's opportunity; these were obviously not generals of any invading force but creatures from another world, country or another island. It mattered not to Green who or what they were but more as to how he could (unknowingly) persuade them to come quietly with him to the Great Hall, where he would present them as prisoners.

"**What do you want?**" Green bellowed.

"You don't have to shout" George replied "just take us to where someone can either get us back home or at least contact our parents." Homes, parents, Green thought, were these creatures just lost. Had he made a big mistake? Was he now going to look very stupid when explaining things, especially the injuries he had (not) sustained from the 'marauding army of invaders'?

Green frantically fought for a solution, when in the distance out of George's line of sight, he saw three other dragons approaching. Dragons White and Grey were closely being followed by Dragon Yellow, who as always, did not want to be at the front line of any danger. Green hatched up another plan, not a very good one, but one that, he thought, might work.

"Look" Green said speaking quickly, "I had to run away earlier for I spotted one of our more annoying dragons, a yellow dragon who just causes loads of trouble and chases us all the time. He's a real pain." Dragon Green, every so often, looked nervously behind him at the three tiny dots of the rapidly approaching dragons. Dragon Green continued "I believe if Dragon Yellow saw you racing towards him shouting and screaming, then I am sure he would run away and leave us alone, you see he is a real coward at heart and avoids any confrontation." Green spied the three dragons getting even closer, "Look, there's Dragon Yellow chasing my two friends right now, he really is a nuisance. If you help me, I and my friends will only be too pleased to help you."

George thought this request to be rather strange but everything about the Island of Draegonia was strange and he and his cousins were not in a position to reject any form of help. "What do you want us to do?" George said as he was joined by his three pals. "Just pick up those sticks and hide behind those boulders" Green pointing to several sticks on the ground and gesturing the four back to their camp "And as my two dragon friends get to me, with their assistance I will try to stop and persuade the Yellow one from annoying us further." Green's plan, although a rather shaky one, was taking shape. "If Dragon Yellow does not take our advice I will guide him to where you will be hiding over there behind those rocks" Green continued in a more urgent voice, whilst pointing again to the boulders. "And, as Dragon Yellow passes, you should all jump out waving your sticks and screaming. It frightened me when you did it and I know it will scare the living daylights out of Dragon Yellow, who as I have told you, is a coward at heart." Green, further to reinforce the logic of his demands, added. "You will teach him a very good lesson which he deserves and will be appreciated by all the other Dragons of Draegonia."

The four children saw the three dragons getting even closer and now having no time whatsoever to discuss things or ask questions, each picked up a stick and hot footed it to conceal themselves behind the rocks of what had been earlier the corner stones of their makeshift camp.

Zach thought the idea of scaring a dragon real cool, whilst Joel was again thinking that if they made friends with the inhabitants of the island he might get a well deserved breakfast. George and Grace took up their positions quite close to each other but well out of sight of the three dragons that they could see running up to Dragon Green. Green appeared to be holding up one of his paws in a gesture to halt the three from proceeding any further. The four saw him speaking and pointing to where they were concealed and laying in wait, but too far away to hear what Dragon Green was actually saying.

Dragon Green had stepped in the path of the oncoming three dragons. **"Stop,"** he commanded, "go no further. I have them cornered and tied up, there was a bit of a fight but this time they were no match for me."

Yellow opened his panting mouth and not to be out done of any glory said, "Yes this is where we cornered them earlier, after I had chased the remnants of their invading force away" "Uh UMM" coughed Green," continuing with his update. "I know nothing about any other soldiers as I was unable to assist Dragon Yellow in dispensing with them. I was concentrating on the capture of the four creatures now safely restrained behind those rocks and I am of the firm belief it was the very same four that set on me yesterday."

Yellow stared in amazement at Green. What was he saying, that he Dragon Yellow had single handed chased the entire invading force away? But before Yellow could think any further, Green ordered: "Look we need to take these four Creatures"...... **"Generals"** Yellow interjected, "Generals, creatures whatever" Green growled, "They need to be taken back to the Great Hall for Dragon Black to deal with." Green knew only too well that Dragon Black would not listen to any of their stories or allegations, they would all be sentenced to immediate 'Volcanic Death', the price paid for all who crossed or upset Dragon Black.

"We'll go and get them" White and Grey said in unison, **"NO"** Green snapped, "It is only fair that as Dragon Yellow has done so much to assist in their capture that he leads them to Dragon Black, it should be his honour." Yellow preened, "Of course Green, I'll go over right away and drag them to and through the streets of Draegonia for all to see how **we** deal with invaders." But with legs visibly shaking Yellow waddled forward, towards where the boulders stood and his future prisoners, he thought, were tightly tied up.

Out of Yellow's earshot, Green spoke quietly to White and Grey, he was about to play his next move. "You know these four creatures are slippery characters. I have had to twice tie them up as they seem able to get loose quite easily and it will be important that we get them into lock ups right away." Green turned to look at Yellow, who was slowly approaching the side of the boulders and a sly grin spread across his face as he started to say, "White and Grey, I suggest that…" Green did not finish his sentence, for as Yellow took the last few steps towards the boulders, four yelling, arm waving, stick wielding, screeching creatures emerged. A startled Dragon Yellow took immediate fright, turned and ran for his life chased even harder by the four who had gained confidence that they were in no danger and just doing what Dragon Green had told them to do. Dragon Yellow running at speeds several times faster than the pursuing children shot past the three dragons. Green took the initiative. "Stay here you two, leave it to me." And with that, ran towards the four young warriors. As he neared them, Green put on a false smile and said how pleased he was with their efforts. "You certainly showed him a thing or two, well done" Green congratulated. "Now" he continued, pointing to the ground. "Throw your sticks down here and sit down and do not move, just wait for me whilst I explain to the other two dragons that you need and deserve our help.

The four immediately dropped their make shift weapons and sat together on the ground as Green had instructed. Green returned to where White and Grey were looking on in amazement at the remarkable event of Green single handed stopping the young warriors and disarming them.

Meanwhile, George turned to Grace and showing considerable concern whispered. “I don’t know what is going on but things seem to be rather strange. I don’t like this one bit. Why are we sitting here with them over there, where has that yellow dragon gone and what are those three cooking up?”

Green was indeed cooking up a plan. “OK you two, White you inform Dragon Brown that we have recaptured the ‘Generals’, Grey, you go after Yellow and stop him from making a fool of himself and be quick about it.”

Both dragons acknowledged Green and set off in different directions. Green had now rid himself of any observers. He definitely did not want any other dragon round him during the next phase of his plan which was to march the four as captives, back to Draegonia, to face the wrath of Dragon Black.

Dragon Grey ran as fast as he could and finally caught up with Dragon Yellow just as he was entering the city limits. “Hey hold up Yellow, stop running!” Yellow skidded to a halt. “Where are they? What’s happened to the other two? Are they alive?“ he said shakily.

“Oh, you should have been there. Dragon Green was marvellous he stopped those creatures from chasing you, forced them to lay their weapons down and even made them kneel before him.” Grey knew he had exaggerated very slightly but Dragon Grey was usually very boring, had little conversation and never got things totally right, just like now.

Yellow was impressed, but fearing that Dragons Grey and White would see him as a coward, wanted to put the record straight and get his version across.

"I wasn't running away from them you know, but seeing that they had escaped and had weapons I was not going to take any chances and was running to get re-enforcements." Grey knowing this not to be true just ignored Yellow's protestations and said, "Look we need to inform Dragon Black of the situation and that the creatures have been captured."

Yellow nodded furiously. "You're right and we can confirm that all the others have left the island as they are now in fear of us." Yellow was thinking fast on his feet as he had not seen any others and remembering what Green had said to White and Grey knew that everyone would believe he had chased them away. Yellow thought of the medal and honour that would be bestowed on him by Dragon Black, then momentarily he shuddered at the thought of what Dragon Black would do to him if the true situation was found out and that he had told lies.

It was just dawning on Yellow that Green, whilst giving him all the credit, was also making him seen as the dragon who was responsible for reporting an army that was not there and running away when tackled by four very small creatures. Yellow's concerns were soon, at least for the time present, dismissed, as Dragon Grey confirmed that at the Council of Dragons, Dragon Black had praised both him and Green for their excellent and heroic work. The two dragons were soon within sight of the entrance leading to The Hall of Draegonia and were both thinking of what to say to Dragon Black as they entered his council chamber.

Meanwhile, Dragon White had just arrived at police headquarters where Blue and Brown were in deep conference. "White," Brown demanded taking off his reading specs and peering into White's eyes, "what have you to report?" Dragon White had always been impressed by Brown and today felt that Brown should be told the whole story from the beginning and that although the creatures had appeared to have attacked Dragon Yellow, who she had always considered a bit of a weakling, now believed the creatures were actually quite small and really not a threat to any dragon.

"**AHtisshooo**" White let out an almighty sneeze showering all around with more sticky black spots. Dragon Blue, who had not recovered fully from the last sneeze of Dragon White, wiped his front and face peering at him in disgust. "Once you have made your final report you had better get yourself off to the hospital. You're no good to anyone with that cold" he said.

Brown, wanting just the facts, ignored everything. "Look," he said "what is your report?" White took a deep breath and informed of the events leading up to Dragon Green's re-capture of the creatures that Green had said were the ones previously responsible for his beatings and injuries. White also informed of Green's intention to bring in the General's (Creatures, Children, whatever they were called) to be locked up and that Brown and Blue should prepare for their imminent arrival. Dragon Blue jumped up. "Right, the cells are prepared and ready I will arrange for extra officers to be on hand!" Brown, still with a frown on his face, looked at White and asked "And what about the weapons they used, are they chemical and have they been secured, and have we the antidote?"

White looked totally blank, She had an idea that her sneezing could be the cause of 'Flame Outs' and that possibly, she had got the disease not from chemical warfare, but a combination of swallowing huge amounts of sea water and a strange type of seaweed that had been ignited by some form of missile fired by the strangers earlier. "I only saw them use sticks" she hastily replied. "And I never got close enough to their camp to see if they had anything like chemical weapons and I don't really know what an antidote looks like."

"Enough of your whimpering," Brown retorted. "Get yourself off to the hospital and have a thorough check up, we will await Dragon Green and the prisoners." With no more to say, White bounded out of the police station into the bright sunlight, worried that she had still not been able to have the courage to tell of her earlier encounters with the prisoners, now being brought in by Dragon Green.

# Chapter 12

## Imprisoned

Dragon Green had made superficial friendship with the four, what Green referred to as 'the Generals'. Although he knew there was never any real army and that Dragon Yellow would most probably get the blame for the misinformation, Green wanted to make Brown the real scapegoat. Dragon Brown had never trusted Green and there was bad feeling between them, mainly on Green's part. Green was now entering the last phase of his plan to take Dragon Brown down.

Firstly, he had to win the confidence of the four children standing in front of him. Secondly he had to establish what the true facts were if he was to weave them into the story he had to concoct and present. "So what are your names? He asked. The four children answered in turn. Dragon Green fired question after question.

"What are you doing on this Island and how did you get here? What weapons do you have? Are there others? Where is your landing craft? How did you destroy our flames?" These were just a few of the questions Green raised. The four children co-operated providing concise and accurate answers, telling Green they had nothing to hide and that they had no idea that dragon flames had been destroyed. After a short time and with a benevolent smile and reassurance from Green, they once more collected all their things and headed off to where Dragon Green promised help. After some time they approached the steepest part of the island, having to walk around a narrow ledge leading to the plateau of Draegonia and the home of all the dragons.

Green raised his claw hand and halted the group, suggesting they had a rest before tackling the difficult track ahead that narrowed and ran round the volcano's steepest part. Green pulled a long rope from one of the children's bags and knowing that George and Grace were the ones in charge, suggested that they consider the dangers ahead. "Look" said the Green pointing to the steep drop below, "I think it would be a sound and safe decision for each of you to tie yourselves round the waist and let me walk ahead with the rope tied to my tail. If anyone then slips the rope will save them" George and Grace both saw the sense in the suggestion and allowed Dragon Green to tie the blue nylon rope round each of them and pass a longer yellow one through, linking them altogether just like climbers do.

What George found worrying was that the dragon insisted that the right hand of each of the children should also be tied to the rope. "Why do we have to have our hand tied?" George demanded. "Well," said the dragon, "It saves you time if something did happen. Rather than trying to grab the rope, the rope is more readily to hand." With that the dragon pulled hard on the lead rope forcing each child in turn to take a step forward. Dragon Green quickened his pace; the children clearly now prisoners, dragged at great speed, they soon rounded the precipice and were in sight of the City of Draegonia.

Dragon Brown was taking in the late afternoon summer sun and looking in the distance towards the main route into Draegonia could see Dragon Green with a line of small creatures behind him. "Good grief!" he exclaimed. "The blighter has done it; he has captured them and is bringing them in."

Dragon Blue arrived at Brown's side with two other dragons (Pale and Light Blue) behind him. They were Dragon Blue's senior constables whom he relied upon for special occasions. All four dragons watched as the procession neared.

Green was now pulling hard on the rope that tightly held the four and as their right hands ware all firmly disabled, they had no chance of undoing the rope and escaping. They all knew that things were bad and that instead of them being helped they were now in deep trouble and that Dragon Green was a liar and certainly no longer to be trusted. Unfortunately the realisation that was too late to stop them being dragged towards four important looking dragons standing outside a blue painted section of the volcano face, with a cave entrance displaying the sign of a 'Police Station'.

"Thank goodness" Grace shouted above the noise of cheering that got louder by the minute as more and more differently coloured dragons came out of door like holes, all cheering and clapping Dragon Green. "We haven't done anything" Grace protested. George shouted "Look we are friendly and just need help and this green dragon has tied us up for no reason." The crowd of dragons grew larger, dividing into two lines either side of the street as Green violently dragged the four through the channel of surging onlookers, towards Dragon Brown.

Brown spoke and as he did so the cacophony of grunts, groans, growls and cheers, of all the dragons abruptly stopped, so that everyone could hear him. "Well done Dragon Green, capturing such a dangerous looking mob must have taken some real courage." Brown was not sincere in his remarks as he quickly surveyed four very distraught youngsters.

Green, with the crowd obviously on his side took the initiative and replied "Thank you Dragon

Brown, it was no more than **you** ordered." Brown noted the sarcasm and not wishing to have a public debate turned to Dragon Blue. "Untie these creatures, take them into the station and provide them with food and water. They look as though they need it." Blue reminded Brown that Dragon Black was insistent that anyone caught was to be placed in individual cells for interrogation. "Yes, yes" Brown said with some agitation, "But not now. It is very hot and if we are not careful we shall all be crushed by so many dragons all trying to look at the prisoners. We also need to get all evidence and information first, before we do any interviewing." Blue cut the ropes and with his two assistants marched the four children inside the station and to where one uncomfortable cell awaited for each of them.

Grace, George, Zach and Joel all fought and struggled but the dragons were far too strong for them. "George." Grace shouted. "Have you noticed that all the dragons have black spots, just like the ones that appeared on the Green one?" George was not interested in Grace's observation for he, unceremoniously, was being thrown into a large damp, very black cell that was only punctuated with a sliver shaft of light passing through a very narrow slit of a window high on the rocky wall. Behind him the cell door of thick granite rock slid into place. These cells were designed to hold dangerous dragons, not small children. There was no escape.

Each of the children had similar cells and the food and water ordered by Dragon Brown was nowhere to be seen. The intrepid four were all hungry, thirsty, tired, frightened and now well and truly locked up.

Dragon Green was still receiving praise and adoration from the vast crowd of dragons that had gathered outside the Draegonia Police Station. Green was finding the constant back slapping rather painful as dragons showed their appreciation by using their tails instead of clapping their paws together.

Green moved quickly, he needed to see Dragon Black and get his story straight. Yellow could take the praise for chasing away the army of invaders that Green now knew had never existed. Green had the creatures, believed by everyone to be the 'Generals' or leaders. Green further calculated that it was Dragon Brown who was in charge and it was Dragon Black who ordered him and Dragon Yellow to capture the four, who were all safely locked up.

Green also knew it was Dragon Black's wish for the prisoners to be interrogated immediately and right now he had important information which would be the undoing of Dragon Brown.

## Chapter 13

# Green, Envy & More Deception

As Dragon Green approached the Great Hall's main entrance he could hear Dragons Yellow and Grey discussing the recent events with Dragon Black.

"**SO**," Dragon Black spoke in a gruff and very loud growl "the invaders have been repelled thanks to the bravery of Dragon Yellow and those commanding them have been apprehended after a brave struggle by Dragon Green. Where are they now?" Just as Yellow was about to reply, Green very casually but with an air of superiority, ambled in.

"I have handed them over to Dragon Brown for interrogation" Green reported, "and they are now securely all locked up in the cells." Dragon Green was full of himself. He knew he would be seen as the dragon that had taken the initiative and followed the strict orders given to him by Dragon Black.

"As commanded by you Dragon Black and after a further struggle, I managed to apprehend and disarm the creatures, just as they ambushed and attacked Dragon Yellow."

Yellow interjected. "Yes, they did attack me, ambushed me, were going to kill me, but I eluded them." Yellow did not want Dragon Black to know he had in fact run away. Yellow continued. "Earlier, I reported to Dragon Green other important intelligence concerning the failed invasion and met up with Dragon Grey to report back, as instructed, to you Sir." Yellow was again bending the truth but both Dragon Grey and Green just nodded.

Dragon Black looked down from his throne where he surveyed all of the Great Hall, "How did you manage to capture them, Green?" Black quizzically asked. Green was not ready for this question so soon and thinking on his feet he explained, "Well, on seeing me again and knowing that I had fought them off earlier they, knew they were no match for dragons and surrendered as soon as they saw me running to defend Dragon Yellow."

"That's right," Grey said, "I saw it all. Dragon Green was magnificent, he just went straight up to those terrorists, raised his claws, pointed to the ground and they threw their weapons down and kneeled before him."

Dragon Black snarled. "Well done Green, so what of the weapons they used to destroy our ability to spit fire?" "I made them carry back everything they had with them Sir," Green reported.

Dragon Green was delighted with the way things were turning out. Soon he would have Dragon Brown's job of Chief of the Army. He was about to stitch Dragon Brown well and truly up.

Green, cocking his head to one side in a questioning manner, continued: "Brown has taken full command of all the perpetrators and their equipment is held at the station. Do you wish for me to bring it here for you, Dragon Black?" Black stretched his wings and bringing them back to his side, opened his very large jaws, gulped a mass of air and breathing out tried and failed to shoot his flame. Dragon Black's ability to strike fear through his enormous flame throwing expertise was no more, he too had lost his most fearsome weapon.

Black did not want anyone to be a threat to him and his most urgent goal now was how he could quickly obtain the ability to spit fire from his huge mouth before anyone else could.

"Green, take Dragon Yellow with you and bring to me all the equipment taken from the prisoners. Grey," he continued "you go and position yourself at the northern lookout point and report to me immediately if the invaders should return." Then, with three mighty thrashes of his tail, Dragon Black thumped the ground, sending echoes throughout the cavernous and numerous corridors of Draegonia's seat of power.

Yellow moved swiftly to the main exit backing all the way, not wishing to offend Dragon Black by turning his back on him. Green yanked Yellow's tail. "Come on let's be quick about it. We have more work to do!"

Green and Yellow exited the Council of Dragons as the sun was sinking in the West, a ball of glowing red fire heading below the far and distant horizon. Soon it would be dusk and Green wanted to finalise the destruction of Brown's reputation and position.

"Look Yellow," Green said, "you have had a tough day and I know that Dragon Brown will want you to make a full written report before you can turn in." Yellow nodded, thinking that all he wanted to do now was find a place to curl up and sleep. After all he had fought off an army, helped capture some fearsome generals of an invading force and been praised for his efforts by Dragon Black, this was a day for him to remember and it was through the help of Dragon Green that his 'Heroic Deeds' had been recognised.

"But Dragon Brown will want my report first," Yellow exclaimed.

"Yes, but not necessarily in person, Yellow" Dragon Green was again hatching yet another devious plan. "Why not give me your written report and I will take it with me to save you time and inconvenience of attending in person?" Green suggested.

"But I don't know how such a report should be written or the type of information it should contain" Yellow moaned. Green sat on his haunches, and from one of his pouches (that all dragons have within their folds of skin) pulled something that looked closely like paper and a pen. "Yellow, you tell me what you saw and did and I will write it for you."

Green rose up and went over to where a large tree cast a shadow from the sinking sun and within its shadow sat down on a seat made out of volcanic rock. Green then with pen in claw started to write. "Yellow," he said, "When and where did you first see the invading army retreat?"

Yellow answered that he was uncertain. "How many were there?" Green continued.

"I'm not sure." Yellow was confused. He knew he had told everyone that he had seen the invaders leave but in all honesty could not recall seeing them.

"Dragon Green," Yellow spoke in a nervous whisper, "I am exhausted, it has been a tiring day and you know what happened probably better than me and anyhow I am just no good at expressing myself and well," Yellow paused, "I just am no good at writing."

Green, not wanting Yellow to say any more, interrupted him and said: "Oh, OK if you're asking me to help you write it, let me see, the events went something like this" and he began to speak as he wrote.

*Report of Events*

*Today I was ordered by Dragon Black to support Dragon Green in verification of the strength and position of the invaders that appeared to have made camp due south of our City, reported by Dragon Green who had seen a number of moving lights the previous evening.*

*Dragon Green had gone to investigate on his own and had been attacked by four creatures, most likely terrorists, and returned injured with his report. Dragon Brown was provided with full information and had determined there must be hundreds if not thousands of invaders. Following a meeting and the bequest of Dragon Black it was agreed for me (Dragon Yellow) and Dragon Green to investigate further and report back.*

*Early this morning Green and I crept up to where the lights seen the previous evening had come from. We split up to gain as much and useful intelligence as was possible. Dragon Green took on the task of capturing those who we believed to be in command and I sought out where the main army was located. Following my natural instincts I saw that the army was in fact departing and that just a few stragglers remained. On seeing me running towards them they took fright and ran to their crafts that were departing out to sea. I counted several of these craft and estimate there could have been a thousand or more, but confirm they had now all run off.*

*On returning back to Dragon Green who was joined by Dragon Grey and Dragon White I was ordered by Green to take charge of the prisoners and return back to Draegonia Central. On approaching where Dragon Green had them captive, it would appear that the prisoners had managed to free themselves and on my approach, attacked me. Naturally I was concerned for Dragons Green's, White's and Grey's safety and returned to Draegonia Central with the news and to obtain additional support. But on reaching Draegonia City outskirts, Dragon Grey caught up with me and confirmed that single handed Dragon Green had recaptured the four creatures and was bringing them in and that he did not require any assistance.*

***Signed.*** *Dragon Yellow.*

Green with a broad smile re-read out loud the report and handed it to Yellow with his pen. "Good report, Yellow. They will be proud of you!"

Yellow, not quite knowing what was fact or what was fiction, or who had made up what, hesitatingly held the pen. “Is that what actually happened Green?” He questioned, Green nodded, “Well isn’t it? Did you not see and chase away the few remaining creatures and see them take to their crafts? If not, then you told Dragon Black a pack of lies.”

Yellow grabbed the report, saying as he hurriedly signed it “Look, I have a splitting headache Green, I’m tired and exhausted. It’s all been too much for me and I need to see a ‘Dragon Doctor’ about my nonexistent flame.”

Green, showing some false compassion blinked a couple of times, licked his lips in pleasure as his manipulation of events were really taking shape, waved and pointed his tail in the direction where Yellow lived. “Off you go, leave everything to me; I’ll give YOUR report to Dragon Brown at the same time I make mine.”

“Thank you Green you’re the best dragon friend anyone could have!” Yellow’s departing words fell on deaf ears. Dragon Green was now thinking of his own report and how he was going to implicate Brown and Yellow as incompetent fools. Once more Dragon Green searched the folds of his scaly skin for another paper-like parchment to write **his** report.

*I Dragon Green report as follows*

*I Dragon Green was on lookout yesterday late evening following the report by Dragon White of intruders to our Island and the connection that may be between them and our ability as dragons, to no longer spit fire.*

*During the evening I saw many lights coming from the south and believed it essential for an investigation. I crept towards the lights and heard what could have been many creatures but before I could really determine actual numbers was set upon by at least four. They used clubs and sticks and caught me by surprise resulting in a number of injuries. Deciding that it was more important to return to Draegonia Central and report I did no more than fight off the attackers and returned as expediently as my injuries would allow.*

*I reported to Dragon Brown that I had seen some lights and the small number of creatures that attacked me. Dragon Brown informed me that there were hundreds of these creatures and that we needed to report to Dragon Black for further instructions.*

*The Council of Dragons ordered me and Dragon Yellow with some minimum support to proceed to capture the invaders' commanders/generals or anyone in command and report on numbers and weapons the invaders may have.*

*Dragon Yellow was charged with the task of surveying the size and whereabouts of the mass army and reported that he had chased away some stragglers of a vast army that had already decided to depart Draegonia.*

*My role was to identify and apprehend the invaders, believed to be the commanders, spotted by me hiding in a camp site by the second southern most ledge of open ground some four Dragon Miles from the City.*

*Despite these terrorists putting up a fight, they were no match and insignificant against my onslaught. They were subsequently captured and tied up. They are clever creatures though and twice they managed to break free requiring further apprehension by me. These perpetrators were under restraint when Dragons White and Grey were sent to assist.*

*I requested Dragon Yellow to take charge of the prisoners and return to Draegonia Central. But, before he could reach where they had been left fully tied up, they had broken free and attacked him. As a consequence Yellow, I believe was frightened and was seen to run off by Dragons White, Grey and I. Seeing the urgency of the situation I launched myself at all four perpetrators and on seeing me approaching they immediately surrendered.*

*I sent Dragon Grey after Dragon Yellow and ordered Dragon White to return with the updated intelligence. I then secured the prisoners and marched them back to Draegonia Central and placed them into the custody of Dragon Brown requesting they be immediately placed in cells for interrogation. All equipment that was found in the prisoners' camp was made to be carried back by them and held by Dragon Brown and awaiting further investigation. However, I believe that there is more to the foiled invasion and that we may well have a traitor in our midst. I question why and how is it that all dragons have 'Flame out' and if Dragon Yellow is correct in reporting the invaders have left in crafts, where are they now, will they return and what plan has Dragon Brown got to defend us? I am also concerned that Dragon Brown is showing a complete lack of urgency in this matter.*

*It is my recommendation that we appoint a younger and more energetic dragon as head of the Draegonia Army as Commander in Chief.*

**Signed.***Dragon Green*

Dragon Green read his report to himself out loud and grinned. He was taking a mighty risk but he had nothing to lose. Both his and Yellow's report were not going to be handed to Dragon Brown. Green had decided that Dragon Black would immediately react to any thought of a traitor within their midst.

Green also knew that, when he informed Dragon Black that Brown was going to feed and water the prisoners, showing them compassion and not immediately getting down to interrogating them, Black would become distrustful of Brown. It would be easy for Green to suggest that it was Brown who was in fact a traitor, in league with the four prisoners and their invading army, planning to overthrow Draegonia's leadership.

Of course, what Dragon Green did not know was that there were two other dragons that had been in contact with the four children and knew the true facts as to how they had arrived on the island. Green's plan was not foolproof, but of course, this he did not know.

Dragon Blue quizzically looked at Dragon Brown. "Why have we not started the interrogation Brown, what's the holdup?" Brown stroked his chin. "Look Blue" he said, "I just cannot get my head round things. It does not make sense. Firstly the size of these creatures, they are no match for any dragon, including Dragon Yellow, who wants us to believe chased away the remnants of an invading force, who ran away from HIM!"

Blue nodded in agreement, "It is strange," he said.

"Then there is this thing about the loss of our ability to throw flames" Brown moved closer to Blue and whispered, "If I did not know better I would think we are all being taken for fools and that all is not what it seems."

Dragon Blue, seeing the concern on Brown's face and an ever deepening frown, sat bolt upright and with all the authority of a legal representative he could muster, said: "Right Brown, let's look at the facts. Firstly, we have corroborating evidence from four dragons." Blue stood up and paced the room and continued with his assessment. "Dragon White reported we were being invaded yesterday morning and spotted what we can assume was the advance party of three creatures. Then, there is Dragon Green who appears to have been the most heroic of us all, who spotted a camp site, investigated and escaped with actual injuries."

"Umm, that's a matter of opinion and interpretation" Brown interjected.

"Well, interpretation or not we have Dragon Yellow's actual sightings of the forces, his being attacked by the prisoners and then on top of this we have the observations of Dragon Grey." Dragon Blue stopped his pacing and looking straight at Dragon Brown finalised his understanding of events by saying. "Finally, of course there is my sighting the day before yesterday of a weird looking craft approaching the island, I think it was either red or orange in colour. And if that's not enough, every dragon on the island has lost their flame and we now have four prisoners to interrogate."

Brown did not move but raising his head, he just stared at Blue. Dragon Brown could see the facts, he just had nothing to go on, but his instincts told him, something was very wrong.

Dragon Blue made for the door that led to the cells. "Come on Brown, let's talk to the prisoners."

Brown beckoned Blue to stop. "Look, it's been a long day and those four are not going anywhere. Feed them, make them comfortable and we will speak with each one in the morning. Sleeping in a dark cell overnight is enough to persuade anyone to talk."

Blue, somewhat taken aback, stared at Brown, for these comments worried him. "Brown, we go back a long way when our fathers and forefathers could fly and roamed the world but I have never thought you to be the first one to go directly against Dragon Black's orders. Black has ordered us to capture and interrogate, nothing about making the prisoners comfortable or leaving their interrogation until they have had chance to sleep."

A tired Dragon Brown heaved himself up and moving towards the main entrance door, looked back at Blue, smiled and said: "You know that Dragon Black is cold hearted and that for him, interrogation actually means torture. Let's investigate further before we make a mistake we will regret." Brown opened the door onto the deserted street and in parting, waved a salute to Blue. "We are supposed to be professionals

Dragon Blue and should be dealing with this in a professional way."

Blue watched, as Brown marched off up the road as the sun, with its last glowing embers of light, gave way to the full blackness of night.

Dragon Green was once more re-entering the Great Hall feeling somewhat confident and clasping both his and Yellow's written reports tightly within his sweaty claws. He knocked hard on the enormous stone door leading to where Dragon Black was still seated on his throne.

"Sir," Green started, "I require some guidance and advice." Green knew that Dragon Black was positively agreeable to being 'sucked' up to.

"What is it?" Black barked back. "It's late and I have no time for idle chitchat."

"Oh!, your Dragonship," Green responded in a sickly, smothering voice, "I know you have much to do and have little time to waste, but I have some important news concerning the prisoners." Green continued to move nearer to Black bowing and with head down, mumbled "If you're not interested then of course I....." Green was interrupted.

"What are you mumbling about Green, speak up? If it's important spit it out and get on with it, for if you are wasting my time," Dragon Black paused, lowered his head and looking Green full in the eyes, snarled, "You will not only be sorry but possibly may not live to regret your intrusion."

With that, Green placed both reports, he had been so nervously clutching, on a round granite table immediately to Dragon Black's left and in easy reach for him to grab them. "What are these?" Green took a deep breath thinking perhaps this had not been such a good idea. "Sire, your Dragonship, Sir," he whimpered.

"Oh, get on with it, Green" Dragon Black exclaimed as he read Yellow's report first. "These should be given to Dragon Brown." Black once more snarled, his large sharp white teeth periodically being licked by his large, long, blood-red tongue.

Green seeing that Black had fully read Yellow's report stood on his hind legs stretched himself up to full height, (he was still tiny compared to Dragon Black). "I believe we have a traitor in our midst"

Green's comment was immediately jumped on by Black. "Do you know for certain who?" Black was now more than interested and was intently reading Green's report when his eyes fell on the statement;

***"However, I believe that there is more to the foiled invasion and that we may well have a traitor in our midst."***

Black once again placed his ugly and enormous head close to Green's "**Whoooo**" he bellowed, sending shock waves not only through the Great Hall, but so loud and violent was his outburst, he could be heard as far as the police station.

Green, wasted no time "Sir, your Dragonship."

"Oh don't start that again," Black snarled once more, his eyes becoming so fiery they looked like two very red hot coals that with his gaze burnt through to the soul.

"Look Sir, I was told to give my reports only to Brown and, because of events, I was not sure if you would ever see them." Green continued, "We have the prisoners locked up but I overheard Dragon Brown order Dragon Blue that they should be fed and watered and..." Green paused for effect, "**And** he **ordered** for them **to be well looked after**, is that a way to treat terrorists?" Green continued as Dragon Black moved back allowing Green more space to breathe.

"I am also concerned Sir, that Dragon Brown has not done anything to ensure our defences are reinforced, or that sufficient lookout posts have dragons on duty. In fact he appears not to take the situation we are in seriously and I can only presume that he either is incompetent or in league with the invading force."

Black's eyes narrowed. His head was once more close to Green's. "Is that all the evidence you have against one of our oldest and respected dragons?"

Green smiled a sickly grin and holding up outstretched arms replied, "I can only give you the facts and no doubt if Brown is doing everything you have asked..." Green's grin slowly faded and a more menacing look ran across his face. "Brown should have completed the interrogations with a report on your desk by now. As I have said, either Brown is just incompetent or a traitor, but either way should such a dragon be in charge of our defences at a time when you, Dragon Black, need total and unquestioning commitment..." Green paused and then added "...and loyalty?"

Green had played his final card. He knew that Dragon Black had a vicious temper, acted on little information and was highly defensive of his position and authority. No one would be allowed to threaten him or his position as King of Draegonia. Dragon Black pondered, reread Green's report, raised his head and looked down again at Dragon Green. "You have done well Green, but there is one more job I need you to do."

## Chapter 14

# Green Makes an Arrest

At Draegonia Police Station, Dragon Blue had heard the roar that came from the Hall of Dragons earlier. It sent a shiver down his blue spine. He thought of what some poor dragon soul was going to go through as that particular sound came from Dragon Black and always spelt trouble.

Blue had just finished feeding and offering some refreshments to the four prisoners, who he admitted to himself, seemed no real threat and with the exception of the smallest, who said he was going to beat them all up, did seem to be very frightened. Dragon Blue had switched the entrance to the cells lights off and was just about to crouch at his desk and finalise his report for Dragon Black when he heard a knocking at the door.

Blue turned from his desk and went over to the same door where much earlier Brown had departed. On opening Blue was amazed to see Dragon Green standing there. "Good evening Dragon Blue, I have a message from Dragon Black. It's most urgent."

Dragon Blue looked at his watch. It was late and, recognising Green's urgency, he beckoned Green to enter, but Green politely refused. "I'm sorry, but you are required to attend immediately with your report to Dragon Black and importantly the findings of the interrogation that both you and Dragon Brown have no doubt completed."

The shiver that had earlier gone down Dragon Blue's spine reoccurred, but this time making his knees also tremble. He knew Dragon Black had ordered immediate interrogations, he was not entirely happy that Dragon Brown had persuaded him to leave it until tomorrow and now he was having to go to face the music and, worse still, face Dragon Black.

Dragon Brown had reached his cave, concerned that something was not quite right but knowing not what. Similar to all other caves of Draegonia, it was coloured as per the skin of the dragon living there. Brown's bedroom was just large enough for him; his bed was covered with a Karkheh covering on a mattress of fine twigs.

On the lumpy walls were ancient picture carvings and drawings in old frames depicting a dark reddish brown dragon being attacked by a Knight in shining armour, sitting astride a white horse, holding a silver lance. Under each of the pictures was the same title.

## 'George and the Dragon'

Dragon Brown, fatigued from a very exhausting day, had eaten a hurried snack of fish and dragon balls, made himself a cold drink (he had nothing to heat his drink up with) and was fast asleep in dragon dreamland, conjuring up thoughts and images of long ago. His dreams brought back the good times when dragons could fly and the Island of Draegonia was a safe haven for all dragons to live.

Meanwhile, Dragons Blue and Green had hurried to where Dragon Black was now pacing impatiently up and down the Great Hall, every stride resonating throughout. Dragons Blue and Green entered. Dragon Green taking a safe option stood behind Dragon Blue, peering over his shoulder.

Dragon Black hearing them enter his chamber, spun round and hurtled himself towards them. "I expect you have some news for me Dragon Blue, no doubt by now you have interrogated the prisoners and have a full report for me. Let me see it!"

Green smirked as Dragon Blue, somewhat flustered, told Black that he had not had sufficient time and that Dragon Brown needed to investigate further to obtain all information and facts prior to the interviews.

"WHAT?" bellowed Black, "I made it perfectly clear that the 'Generals' were to be captured and immediately interrogated! Who countermanded MY orders?"

Before Dragon Blue opened his mouth Green interjected: "Dragon Brown did not want to interrogate the prisoners."

Blue catching his breath defended Brown's decision by repeating himself. "Dragon Black, we have every intention of interrogating the prisoners and Brown and I believe we just need to investigate some anomalies first. By tomorrow afternoon we shall…"

Blue never had chance to finish. Black interrupted. "Green you are now in charge and you Dragon Blue, you are to go with Green, arrest Brown and place him in the cells." Blue stuttered "Oh...Oh...on what charges?"

Black glared at him "The same charges you will be on if you do not carry out my orders Dragon Blue." Black continued, his face displaying a look of thunder. "Brown is to be charged with Incompetence, dereliction of duty and of being a suspected TRAITOR!"

Blue was just about to lodge another protest but saw Dragon Black with his piercing eyes staring at him ready to perhaps have him arrested too. In response Blue agreed he would arrest Brown immediately but really did not require Green to be in attendance. Dragon Black looked even more terrifying and with an attempt to breathe a rain of fire failing, resulting in a small circular puff of smoke emanating from his open mouth, Green was unable to suppress a snigger.

"Green," barked a very angry and annoyed Dragon Black, "Irrespective of what Blue wants, you are **both** to arrest Brown. Green you are in charge of Draegonia's forces and I am issuing a second state of emergency, **AND Blue** from this moment on **YOU WILL** report to Dragon Green, now go and do your duty!"

Dragons Blue and Green turned and in doing so Green saluted. He had achieved his goal. He had engineered what some would have considered impossible. He had won the trust of Dragon Black, was on his way to arrest Dragon Brown and at last, had Dragon Blue reporting to him. Everyone would now be 'Green with Envy' but not him.

Dragon Brown was rudely awakened by a loud banging on the outside door. He stretched and switched on the 'Dragon light' in his bedroom by turning a black disk that revealed an already lit candle. "Who is it" he bellowed.

Moving across the bedroom floor and through into his lounge he opened his front door where Dragon Blue and Dragon Green were standing. "What on earth do you want, what time do you call this?" Brown demanded, "What has happened, have the prisoners escaped, are there more of them coming?" Brown rubbed his tired eyes and stared at the two of them, waiting for an answer.

"I'm sorry Brown" Blue started to say but was interrupted by an officious Dragon Green. "You're under arrest on the orders of Dragon Black," Green spurted out. "Come quietly or we will use force, won't we Dragon Blue?"

Blue ignored Green's feeble attempt to make an arrest and continued in an authoritative but friendly tone. "I am afraid, Dragon Brown, that we have been sent under a state of emergency order issued by Dragon Black to take you into custody."

Dragon Brown thrashed his tail up and down in anger and looking straight at Dragon Green said, "And on what charges am I supposed to be arrested?"

Dragon Blue, somewhat embarrassed, coughed, cleared his throat and continued. "On the basis of negligence and dereliction of duty and suspicion of being..." Blue paused, swallowed with a large gulp and said the words that visibly stunned Dragon Brown, **"suspicion of being a traitor."**

"Put the cuffs on him Dragon Blue," shouted Dragon Green. Green smirked and preened himself, he was loving every minute.

"Is that necessary Green?" Blue demanded. "I don't think Dragon Brown deserves to be treated as a common criminal dragon, after all nothing has been proved and he has nowhere to run."

Green snatched the cuffs dangling from Blues belt and snapped one bracelet to each of Brown's front paws with the chain between, being linked to a similar pair of bracelet cuffs he also affixed to Dragon Brown's hind legs. "He certainly won't run with those on, now let's get him locked up! Or do you want me to report you to Dragon Black as being uncooperative, Dragon Blue?"

Blue looked at Brown who immediately understood that Green was obviously empowered by Dragon Black and that Dragon Blue was powerless but to do exactly as Dragon Green said.

"OK Green," Dragon Brown spoke in an unhurried commanding officer tone of voice, "Let's go NOW, I need my sleep. I expect we're going to have a very busy day tomorrow Green and I trust you will come to your senses." Green just smirked and pushing Dragon Brown forward made him move slowly, taking very short steps because of his chains, marching him back towards the police station, where he too was to be locked up.

## Chapter 15

# Interrogations and more Lies

All other Dragons of Draegonia were asleep, not knowing what had taken place. That is all dragons bar one. Dragon Pink had spent the whole day as usual walking around the island. She usually came back late, but on this occasion it was very much later as she had visited the spot where the four children had landed on the shore. She had wanted to see for herself where the dingy had been placed and if it was secure. Pink had made her mind up that she was going to assist the four to get back to their home. It was nearly three o'clock in the morning and the police station lights were still on. Why? She thought?

There was a knock on the police station door that made Dragon Blue jump. Now what, who can this be at this time of night? Dragon Green was still interrogating the prisoners wanting to be left alone to do it. Dragon Brown was on his own in one of the more comfortable cells, despite what Dragon Green wished. Dragon Blue was not going to let his friend suffer at the claws of Green.

Here however was yet another visitor to the police station. Blue opened the door and revealed the smiling face of Dragon Pink. "What 'Dragon Time' do you call this? It's late Pink, and you should be at home fast asleep. Why are you here? Is there a problem?" Dragon Pink peered in through the open door and seeing no one else around asked Dragon Blue why he was still on duty. Normally the lights would be off and Dragon Blue in bed fast asleep, so something was up.

"Look, Pink" Blue said rather frustratingly, "we have caught some of the invaders who are responsible for the failure of our flames. They are," Blue continued, "in the cells, being interrogated by Dragon Green who is now Commander in Chief of 'Special Forces', the Army and the Police Force of Draegonia." Blue coughed, "And I am sorry to say we also have Dragon Brown in a cell on the command of Dragon Black, so it has been a very difficult and tiresome day. It's nearly morning and I need you to go."

Pink, opened her mouth in a gasp and in doing so a small jet of yellow and white flame was expelled. "Ah, I see your flame has returned then," Blue exclaimed. **"Returned?"** Pink queried, taken aback by this comment. "I never lost it in the first place Dragon Blue."

Blue dismissed the comment in the same way as he dismissed her. "Look I have no time to stand here chatting with you. I've told you, it's late and you should be home. Just leave and let me get on, good night and good morning!" And with a closing farewell gesture shut the door, returned to his desk and crouched down. It had been a very traumatic day, and he still had to wait for Green.

Dragon Green was in the main cell block. The walls were rough and very wet and because there was little light getting through during the day, the air was musty and damp. This was not a place to spend any time and Green wanted to get away as quickly as possible. He knew however, that he had to go through the paces of being seen or heard to be conducting the necessary interviews with the prisoners.

Zach, the youngest, was the first he was to interrogate. Green carried a flickering light that cast weird and sometimes frightening shadows on both walls and across the very high ceiling. The shadows danced menacingly from wall to wall with shapes of ogres, goblins, dragons and fearsome giants. On entering Zach's cell Green first asked for Zach's name. Zach, very angry at being dragged and locked up that afternoon, refused to speak.

Green gave one of his sickly smiles and said, "Look, I really am here to help you. I didn't want to have you captured and treated like criminals but I was under orders, mainly because you and your friends are responsible for us dragons losing our flames."

Green had planned to be nice in order to find out about the antidote urgently required by Dragon Black. Zach turned his back on Green. "I'm not talking to you. You know my name we all told you them earlier and I don't trust you one bit!" Zach was not showing that underneath his bravado he really was shaking with fright. "Anyway, you're going to get everything you deserve Mr Dragon!" Zach said angrily "When George and Grace finish with you, you'll be trussed and stuffed ready for a Christmas dinner!"

Green, realising he was not going to get anywhere with this creature, exited the cell, leaving it once more in pitch blackness. He moved cautiously through the dimly lit corridor to the second cell holding Joel.

Green had exhausted himself and in the darkness, broken only by the flickering flames of Green's portable light. He entered the cell containing Joel but failed to see Joel lunge at him.

Joel kicked, punched and yelled, "Let me out of here! I'm not going to talk to you unless I can have something to eat and drink!" Joel, even though being locked up in the dark, thousands of miles from home and facing his capturer, which was a green dragon, was still thinking of his stomach.

Dragon Green demanded Joel's name and this time, with more direct and aggressive questioning, ordered him to tell how the dragons' flames might be restored. Without any pause or giving time for his prisoner to really answer, Dragon Green rained down a barrage of questions. Green had absolutely no interview technique whatsoever and failed dismally to get any response from Joel, who just scowled at his capturer.

Green realising that he was getting nowhere with the youngest ones, slammed the heavy door of the cell, locking it behind him. He moved on to cell three.

Opening the door he saw Grace standing upright and squarely in front of him, her arms folded and glaring. She was steely eyed and although very tired knew she had to negotiate rather than give in to a scheming dragon. Showing no fear she spoke in a very determined voice "What are we supposed to have done, why are we here and who is responsible for our imprisonment?"

Green once more fired his questions, one after another in rapid succession, requesting her name, age, what she was doing on the island and what was used to destroy the dragons' flames? Ignoring Green's threatening posture and tone, Grace sidestepped all the questions and reiterated her own. The tables were being turned. Green was no match for this stubborn young girl who wanted answers and wanted them immediately.

"So, if you were supposed to be our friend why did you trick us?" Grace, not waiting for an answer, then demanded: "Who is in charge, I want to see them, I want food and water and to be released straight away. That's it. I will not talk to you anymore, whatever you try to do to make me."

With that last outburst, she turned in a show of defiance, with her back towards Dragon Green. Green thought for a moment, should he try torture? But he was worried that, because all four prisoners really did not know what was happening and why, they would not reveal anything anyway.

"So what species are you, at least tell me that?" Green puffed, he was now feeling tired with all the chasing and having to use his brain to make up so many stories. Stories and untruths that he was beginning to lose track of, not knowing what he had said to whom and what the prisoners in his charge would say.

These four were going to be dangerous if he could not manipulate them to go along with what he needed everyone to believe. Looking at the young spirited girl, who still had her back to him, Green decided to call it a day, give up and question the last of the group held in Cell 4.

George was trying to piece all the events together. He knew that these dragons believed the four were responsible for something serious. He had overheard the dragons speak about invaders and generals and of those who had lost the ability to spit flame.

The door to George's dingy and damp smelling cell opened and in walked a very tired and fed up Dragon Green. George taking one look at Green went on the offensive. "You look exactly as I feel, **fed up!**" George continued: "You know you're going to look very stupid once everyone learns that you tricked us in order to lock us up, that we are innocent and are no more than four children washed up on your island after a terrible storm that wrecked our sailing boat."

Green listened to the verbal onslaught of George and realised that if these 'Children' spoke at length with Dragons Blue and Gold, his deceit and lies might well be found out. He had to move fast and these four had to be dealt with before daybreak, or at least before the majority of the Dragon Council could speak with each of them.

"So you are a race of 'Children' sent to invade our peaceful island using a weapon to which there is no antidote!" Green was speaking out a loud not necessarily for George's benefit but more as a rehearsal for what he was going to report to Dragon Black. "On seeing the size and strength of Draegonia Dragons and our fighting expertise…" he was thinking of his reporting about overpowering four attacking Generals ... "your main force ran to get reinforcements, leaving you to spy on us."

George shouted: "Rubbish, that's a pack of lies and who are these Generals who supposedly attacked you?"

"You four, of course; it was after I went to the aid of Dragon Yellow whom you scared away." Green rambled on: "In fact you're the same mob who attacked me the day before, when I wasn't looking and beat me with clubs."

George expelled a loud irritated sigh. "You're saying that four young children jumped you and beat you up?" George laughed showing some disgust at the preposterous allegation, saying: "If anyone believes that fairy story, they must be either very stupid or you must be a very weak dragon. Look at yourself, are you really trying to say we not only attacked you, but actually won the fight?"

George then rubbed salt in the wound: "I suppose you ran off like your friend the yellow dragon. Are all dragons on this island cowards and liars?"

Green roared and as he did so coughed up several circular rings of bluish grey smoke that drifted upwards. "You might think you are clever," Green snarled at George, "but when Dragon Black receives my interrogation report, you and your friends will not be laughing anymore. In fact, make the most of it, for you have little time to live!"

Green turned and foolishly blew out the candle. As he closed the cell door behind him and entered the very dimly lit corridor, he stubbed his left foot on a bucket that 'Dragon Cleaners' had left behind. The metal bucket was kicked high into the air. Green let out a roar of pain, which was doused by the noise made by the metal bucket bouncing from side to side as it clanged along the corridor.

The noise of Dragon Green's roar and the loud noise made by the bouncing metal bucket startled Dragon Blue. He thought the four prisoners were being given the third degree and felt rather sorry for them. Just as he was about to raise himself up from his crouched position, Dragon Blue saw Green appear. Dragon Green was flustered and looking in some pain. "What's up Green? Is it all over, have you made them talk?" Blue asked.

"Yes," winced Green rubbing his foot. "I have determined that these creatures are extremely dangerous and not to be underestimated." Green, with his back to the wall, crouched down opposite Blue and dragging a wooden storage crate nearby, placed his injured leg on it.

"These creatures are devious and clever. They have stated that **they were assisted** by Dragon Brown and

I will let Dragon Black determine his fate." Blue raised both eyebrows and frowned, but Green continued. "One of them called George, managed to get hold and threw a steel bucket at me, but his aim was poor. Instead of hitting my head, he caught my leg. Just look at the injury," Dragon Green said, pointing to where the bucket he had stupidly kicked had hit him.

Blue got up, went to the first aid box and handed a 'Dragon Plaster' to Green who duly placed it over his wound. "You know Green," Blue said, raising one eyebrow, "You heal very quickly, don't you? Looking at your head, the wound you had yesterday has totally healed, so the cut on your leg will I am sure heal just as quickly."

Green somewhat speedily put his foot on the floor and asked Blue for some 'Dragon Paper' so that he might write his report. Blue opened his desk draw pulled out two sheets and handed them to Green. "Here you are, Green. But why don't you write it in the morning when you are fresh and perhaps not in as much pain?"

"No, it has to be now," Green replied, "whilst everything is fresh in my mind. I don't want to make any mistakes." As his lying words were replaced by silence, Green put 'Dragon Pen' to 'Dragon Paper' and concocted a pack of lies and fictitious events, into an official report, that would mean certain death for all prisoners, including Dragon Brown.

**_Interrogation Report._**
**_For the attention of Dragon Black._**
**_Dragon Date 160/2011._**

*Under the authority of Dragon Black a full interrogation was undertaken throughout the late night and the early morning of the 159/160.*

*The four prisoners admitted they were a species called Children from a distant land they called England but believed to be Britannia who with an expedition force was to invade Draegonia. Their plan was to incapacitate the ability of all dragons to spit flames and to capture the Leader of Draegonia.*

*A struggle ensued during the interrogation when one of the 'Children' called George threw a steel bucket in an attempt to escape. He was overpowered and I suffered some minor injuries during his apprehension.*

*Further questioning revealed that there is no antidote to the chemicals they used and they continue to deny any involvement unless placed under duress or torture. They are clever little creatures that make you believe they are no more than the survivors of a shipwreck. This I have established is untrue and that their landing craft is still somewhere on the island.*

*It has been verified by me, although they constantly deny this unless tortured, that their contact on*

*Draegonia was Dragon Brown, who wants to overthrow Dragon Black.*

*They have also stated to me that they are to send regular signals (by way of a mirror) and that if no such signal is received after a two 'Dragon Day' period, then they will be assumed dead.*

*My recommendation is that the four invaders designated as 'Children' should be tried and sentenced as a matter of urgency, as an example set to others, who may think of attempting to overthrow the leadership of Draegonia.*

*My final recommendation is that Dragon Brown should be tried for treason and that all trials should be undertaken as a matter of urgency in order that we can concentrate on the need to defend Draegonia from any further attack.*

Dragon Green signed the report and was about to fold it when Dragon Blue spoke. "I would like to see the report please." Dragon Blue without asking again plucked the report out of Green's hands and quickly read it.

"Umm, you have established these facts and I suppose you are now going to write them into a statement for the perpetrators to sign?" Dragon Green grabbed the report back, saying that he was instructed by Dragon Black to interrogate and report, nothing about statements from the prisoners.

Blue listened and then said in an authoritative voice, as he once more snatched the report out of Greens sweaty claws, "I'll use a copy of your report Green and will make out the relevant statements; we must uphold due process of law, mustn't we?"

Blue marched over to the 'Dragon Copier' and placed it in for a duplicate to be made. A long pointed beaked bird moved its head from side to side rapidly reading the original and placing its beak intermittently into an ink like liquid to copy a replica onto similar type parchment.

Having made a copy, Dragon Blue gave the original back to Green. "I think we all need to get some shuteye, don't you Green?" Dragon Blue opened the station door and gestured for Green to leave, closing it behind him with a thud.

Green trotted up towards the Hall of Dragons. He had no intention of sleeping, he was intent on doing away with both Brown and the Children, but of course, he now needed the assistance and willingness of Dragon Black.

Within the Dragon Hall, Black was still on his throne but during the night it converted to a strange looking yet fully functional and practical bed.

The high back of the plinth tilted rearwards and a marble slab, drawn out of a compartment usually concealed within the bottom, gave the whole thing sufficient length for Dragon Black to lie on at full stretch.

Green had been admitted through security by a very annoyed dragon who had not expected his unauthorised 200 winks of sleep to be interrupted.

"Wait here!" Dragon Indigo pointed to the official waiting room. "I'll go and see if Dragon Black will see you, but your visit had better be life or death, otherwise it will be literally your death for disturbing him at this hour of the morning."

Dragon Indigo quietly slid off, leaving Green rehearsing how he would present his report, made up of lies, to Dragon Black.

## CHAPTER 16

# Sentenced to Death

Earlier, Dragon Pink had left Dragon Blue at the Police Station; she was very confused and worried for the four now locked up, recalling their story of events.

She had not found them to be in command of an invading force. She had seen no army and she certainly had not seen them carry any weapons. What was she to do? She knew that no one would believe her without proof of the innocence of the four. Suddenly she recalled that the Children had told her of the meeting with Dragon White and that they had been scared into firing a pistol used to send distress flares. Dragon White was an important witness and could be instrumental in helping to free the locked-up four.

Pink decided to act and ran as fast as she could to White's cave. Her head projected forward, her neck outstretched and her little legs carrying her body so fast that she looked like a jet fighter flying low level.

On reaching White's cave, Pink crashed into the entrance door with a thud. White on hearing the crash immediately awoke and rushed to open the door to reveal a slightly dazed Pink dragon. "What on earth are you doing Pink?" White quizzed.

Pink, brushing herself down, pushed past White and entered a very bright white room filled with items taken or collected from the beach. There were plastic bottles filled with coloured water decorating old wooden chests washed up from shipwrecks of bygone years. On two of the walls were hung slightly ragged flags of white with a red cross and a second coloured blue, green and red.

"Quick shut the door, there is a big problem!" Pink crouched on one of the wooden chests and started to update White about the fact that the police station cells now not only held the four children but also Dragon Brown. Pink explained that she had seen the children during the night of the previous day and befriended them. They had told her about their sailing boat mysteriously being caught in a storm, the events on being washed up on Draegonia and the fact that they had seen Dragon White.

White listened intently and went to a tap in the wall and poured hot water into two mugs. The water came from a pressurised ground fissure that collected rain water and when the tap was opened the water passed close to the heated rocks of the volcano. "Dragon Tea" White said.

Pink nodded and took one of the mugs and sipped. White was more than relieved to find she could talk openly about the encounter she had with the four little ones. "You know, I was rather foolish in not explaining things but felt stupid at falling over and skidding into the sea, swallowing all that water and seaweed, and then having to explain myself to everyone."

White paused for a second or two then putting her mug of hot 'Dragon Tea' down grabbed Pinks left paw. "What I cannot understand Pink is why your four friends should attack Dragon Green and cause him so many injuries. I also do not understand why they chased Dragon Yellow." White gasped. "Unless of course Green has lied about the whole thing and that Dragon Yellow is in cahoots with him!"

Pink nodded. "But why lock up Dragon Brown?" She said.

White had no immediate answer but told Pink that they needed to go together to tell Dragon Blue everything. Pink was uncertain. She questioned whether or not Dragon Blue would believe them and if they would be seen as making up stories.

White looked sternly at Pink. "Look Pink, I made the mistake of not telling everyone exactly what happened, I allowed what was a slight exaggeration to become a major lie and as such we now have five facing the wrath of Dragon Black."

Pink agreed saying: "Well I am sure that if we speak to Dragon Blue he will know exactly what to do, so shall we go now?"

White looked at the 'Dragon Clock' on the wall, a peculiar piece of engineering made out of bits of metal, wire, string and wood, but told accurate 'Dragon Time'. "I think we need to go together first thing in the morning and in the meantime you can sleep here tonight."

Pink accepted the offer as White pointed to the spare cave room. Whilst Pink was settling down for what little remained of the night, White washed and dried the mugs, returned to her bed and with one dragon puff blew out the light. Morning would soon come.

Dragon Green was in deep conversation with Dragon Black, who at first was unimpressed at being wakened at such a very late time. His sleep had been disturbed and he was even more irritable than usual. He read Green's, report of the interrogation. Black stopped at the point where it said;

***'It also appears, although they constantly deny unless tortured, that their contact on Draegonia was Dragon Brown.'***

Black's eyes darted up and down the report and back and forth to Green. Black's tail was vibrating with temper his nostrils snorted puffs of foul smelling smoke that made Green wince and cough.

Dragon Black boomed out, "THEY ARE ALL TO BE PUT TO DEATH, NOW!"

"Your Dragonship… err … Sir" Green's sickly voice was nervous, he had expected a reaction from Dragon Black, but nothing like the anger he saw before him.

"WHAT" snapped Black?

"Your Lordship," Green squirmed, "Dragon Blue has informed me that he wants due Draegonia justice to prevail and wishes the four," Green paused, "no the five prisoners to face a court hearing and trial."

Dragon Black had little if any patience at the best of times and now his authority was being questioned. His decisions, his rules, his commands, they all were being discussed and overruled. This, he was not going to allow. Dragon Black, with immense hatred in his glaring eyes, was about to issue orders that meant certain and imminent death sentences would be passed.

Dragon Black roared: "IT'S A TRIAL THEY WANT IS IT? THEN LET'S HAVE ONE! ITS JUSTICE DRAGON BLUE WANTS TO SEE IS IT?

THEN MY JUSTICE WILL BE SEEN AND NOT QUESTIONED!”

Black stretched himself up to full height, his wings unfolding and refolding very slowly but creating great drafts of air that swirled the dust, forming mini cyclones.

He again roared at Green: “YOU WILL GO NOW WITH TWO OF MY DRAGON GUARDS AND BRING THE PRISONERS TO THE MOUTH OF THE VOLCANO WHERE I WILL HOLD COURT. YOU ARE NOT TO BE ACCOMPANIED BY ANYONE ELSE. IS THAT CLEAR GREEN? HAVE I MADE MYSELF FULLY UNDERSTOOD?”

Green, legs quivering, nodded. He knew that by taking the prisoners to the mouth of the volcano, Dragon Black had already made up his mind as to what sentence was to be passed. It would be ‘Death by Burning’. All five would, one by one, be pushed unceremoniously into the white molten lava that lay within the depths of the smouldering mouth of Draegonia’s Volcano.

“SO WHAT ARE YOU WAITING FOR?” bellowed Black “GET OUT OF HERE, **NOW!**“

Green quickly turned 180 degrees and ran to where Dragon Black’s personal guards were. Green eyed several and selected two of the meanest looking to accompany him and headed back to where an exhausted Dragon Blue was fast asleep.

Black meanwhile had stomped off along a corridor known only to him. This large tunnel curled steeply up to a large hidden exit close to the mouth of the volcano. Black emerged into the first shimmering rays of the early morning sun as it rose out of the sea to the East. The immediate surrounding area was quite flat with a gentle slope rising to the smoky and very hot mouth of the volcano. Around the edge and protruding into the mouth were 12 very large flat slabs of fire hardened rock that formed the outer ring of a clock face with no hands.

These slabs were designed to hold dragons that were on trial, but today these would be used to hold one dragon and four children, on trial for their lives.

About 15 dragon paces in front of the nearest of the slabs and facing south was a much larger and taller platform. This was not made of rock but jet black marble with white veins running throughout and the top allowed for a perfect platform from which to view any prisoner who might be unfortunate enough to be chained to any one of the 12 sentencing and execution slabs.

The tall marble platform was to be the perch of Dragon Black who was not only the Judge but also the jury. This trial was going to be nothing but UNFAIR.

Dragon Green was totally exhausted. He had been up all night and seeing the sun rise, realised he had not slept for over 24 hours. With the two dragon guards dressed in their Black, Red and White regalia, on which was printed gold dragon motifs, he aggressively hammered on the police station door. The loud repetitive banging not only woke Dragon Blue but also the prisoners and several other dragons close by whose sleep also had been rudely disturbed.

"Open up and be quick about it" demanded Green. The door opened and Green charged past Blue. "Right, I have an order from Dragon Black to immediately take charge of the prisoners and take them to trial."

Blue rubbing his eyes was taken aback and exclaimed. "What, why and where are you taking them? Dragon Gold needs to be informed if he is to Judge the issues and we need to raise a Jury. This is going to take a little time."

Green smirked and in a very condescending growl said. "You have to do nothing, nothing at all, Dragon Black is going to judge the issues and he is arranging the court to sit right now at Volcano Peak." Dragon Blue winced. He knew time was running out and that executions were inevitable if Dragon Black was to pass judgement. Green told Dragon Blue that he had been ordered by Dragon

Black, that the prisoners were to go with him right away and that failure to comply with these orders would mean he too would be arrested. Dragon Blue's shoulders dropped. He had to, although very reluctantly, obey. Taking the keys off their hooks he went with Green to the cells.

The four youngest prisoners were shackled and linked together with heavy chains. Dragon Brown was pulled from his cell by Dragon Black's personal guards, protesting and demanding to know where they all were being taken to.

The two guards ignoring Brown's arguments took their place top and tail of the line of four children and a very annoyed brown dragon. The line of prisoners and their escorts marched through the open door and headed towards the long trek and climb to Volcano Peak.

Dragon Blue looked on. There was little he could do. His lifelong friend Dragon Brown was certainly being taken to his death and with him four small creatures he felt sure were also innocent of their alleged crimes.

The noise and kerfuffle of the prisoners being marched in chains from the police station towards the volcano, together with the noise generated by all the dragons who had lined up two and three deep along the roadside, was ear shattering. Such was the chatter, growls and grunts that the accumulated cacophony of sound woke Dragons White and Pink.

Pink peering out of her bedroom window shouted to White. "We're going to be too late to save them! Look, they are all being marched in chains and they have Dragon Black's personal guards with them!"

White immediately knew the ramifications of the situation and grabbing her bag told Pink to follow her. Both dragons fought their way through the tightly packed crowds until they reached the police station where Dragon Blue was trying to get through on the voice box (telephone) to Dragon Black. Once more his concentration was interrupted. "Oh, White, Pink, sorry but I really haven't the time….."

He was cut short in mid sentence by Pink. "Dragon Blue, White has some very important information for you concerning the so-called invaders." Pink continued with White nodding profusely. "Dragon White didn't tell the whole story and we believe an injustice is being done."

Blue moved quickly and shut the door. "What on earth are you saying? What information have you and why has it taken so long coming forward?" Blue listened intently to both Dragon White's and Pink's accounts. Once they had finished telling the whole saga, Blue crouched down at his desk.

"We still do not know what Dragon Green is playing at and why Dragon Yellow should be involved in this intrigue," he said picking up the 'Voice Box' and blowing down it to get attention. "Put me through to the Mayor, immediately!"

Blue waited and in less than a few seconds he heard the voice of Dragon Gold. "We have a situation, Dragon Gold, and this is a code RED." On hearing this Dragon Gold listened, whilst Blue gave him a short version of the facts he had been presented with.

Dragon Gold asked where the prisoners were and if Dragon Brown was with them. Blue confirmed that they were being taken, as he spoke, to Dragon Black's court and that there was little time. Dragon Gold was overheard to tell Dragon Blue that he was leaving and would be with him in a few minutes and that in the meantime Dragon Yellow was to be found and brought in for questioning as a matter of urgency.

Pink, immediately volunteered that with Dragon White they would find Dragon Yellow and bring him in. Without waiting for Blue to respond they opened and shot out of the door like bullets from a gun.

Yellow, was actually on his way down the street as he passed the convoy of prisoners and gingerly waved at Dragon Green who, upon seeing Yellow, looked the other way and ignored him. Green had completed his cunning plan making him the second most important dragon in Draegonia and no longer required Yellow. Yellow also was caught up in the jostling crowds.

Some minutes had passed when Yellow saw two dragons forcing their way towards him. "Yellow," shouted Dragon White, "you are needed at the police station right away - it's a matter of life and death!" Pink reinforced the urgency by saying, "And we mean right now!"

By the time all three dragons had returned, Blue was in deep conversation with the Mayor, who in his hurry had forgotten to put on his ministerial chain and looked unusually untidy. Dragons Gold and Blue saw Dragons' Pink and White pushing and prodding Yellow into the office. An office, that was now a very cramped meeting point.

"OK Yellow" Blue barked. "If you do not tell us the truth Dragon Brown, is going to be sentenced to death, and if we do not act now perhaps will be executed before we can get to him."

"That goes for the four children!" Pink cried out. "You must tell us the truth."

Dragon Yellow sat down on his haunches, eyes popping out of his head he was seen to shiver as it dawned on him the game was up. “It was Dragon Green,” Yellow started, “he suggested I make up a story so that dragons would not see me as a coward.” Yellow then detailed everything that had taken place. He confirmed that it was he who ran away from four children who he had been told were tied up by Green. He also confirmed that he had not seen any army but thought there had been one as it was Dragon Green who had told him he had seen them.

Dragon Blue wrote down everything Yellow was saying. “We must hurry Blue,” Dragon Gold was becoming agitated, “surely we can leave the administration and form filling until after we prevent Dragon Black murdering them all?” he said.

Dragon Blue was not to be rushed. He was aware of the urgency but also the need to have documented hard evidence if he was to present it to Dragon Black. “I know the seriousness and urgency, Gold” Blue protested at being rushed. “But if we do not have statements with us from Dragons Yellow, White and Pink, then Dragon Black will just throw our protestations out and execute them all.” He paused, then in a serious tone of voice. “And possibly all of us could end up with the same fate. We must present irrefutable proof of innocence.”

Dragon Green had now reached Volcano Peak and anchored each of the prisoners by their chains to the metal rings protruding from each of the slabs of rock. They were all facing Dragon Black who glared and growled at Dragon Brown, but Black just stared in bewilderment at the four small creatures before him.

“This court is in session” Black boomed out, “I will read out the charges brought against you.” Dragon Black had no charge sheet, just the written reports of Green and Yellow.

Black continued, “First I will take the charge of espionage and assisting the enemy, dereliction of duty and placing Draegonia in great danger” Black’s eyes were focussed on Dragon Brown. “How do you plead?” Black waited for Brown to answer.

Dragon Brown made no move but stood straight (well, as straight as he could be being anchored to the rock by his chains).

“Nothing to say eh!” Black motioned his claw in a circular wave, “You’re guilty by default.”

However, before Dragon Black was just about to pass sentence, Dragon Brown spoke. His voice was loud enough to be heard by all, but he did not shout. His tone was firm and precise with no hint of fear. “Dragon Black, this is not a Draegonian judicial court. I am innocent of any of the trumped up charges and if not released into the custody of the law pending the preparation of my defence, then you will be guilty of imposing improper justice."

Dragon Black roared with laughter, sneering at Brown he leaned forward and growled. "I am the Law, I am the Judge and I dispense the Justice here, something you will soon learn. You're GUILTY AS CHARGED!" he finally bellowed. **"And I sentence you to be thrown to your death."**

Brown eloquently spoke once more. "Not only are you making a big mistake, Dragon Black, but it is you who is in contempt of this so called court, dealing with jumped up charges that will be eventually proved false. Irrespective if you sentence me and the other prisoners to death, you will be responsible for our MURDER."

Black was not going to be threatened or made to look a fool in front of his personal guards and Dragon Green. He was not going to have his authority undermined. "Brown, you are guilty, you have been sentenced to death and you will be the first to be executed, crouch down and shut up!" Black waved his claw up and down in a gesture to Brown.

"Now you four," Black turned his attention and gaze on each of the children, one by one. He spoke, his head moving slowly so that his speech was evenly distributed across the four.

"You are charged with espionage." His gaze moved on. "You are charged with attempted murder." He looked at Grace, "You are charged with using chemical warfare." And finally his gaze came to rest on George. "You are charged with invasion and the attempted overthrow of Draegonia. How do you all plead?"

George, standing on the execution plinth looked on by three worried friends said in a loud voice, "None of us are guilty of any crime."

"That's right!" shouted Zach with clenched fists. Although he was youngest he was not afraid of anything and was prepared to show it.

"Shhh," sighed Grace, "Don't annoy him any more than he already is."

Joel, not to be outdone, piped up. "Look we know you have made a mistake but…." Joel was immediately interrupted by Dragon Black who snarled at him to be quiet.

George had been thinking about their predicament for the last 24 hours and during the forced march to Volcano Peak had chance to talk to Grace. They had both agreed that Dragon Green was behind their capture and that he just lied about everything and was definitely not to be trusted. Neither of the two however, could understand Dragon Brown's position in all this and both questioned why he was a prisoner facing what appeared to be trumped up charges.

Grace had an idea and shouted at Dragon Black. "You have the wrong dragon in front of you facing the wrong charges!"

Black, with his piercing eyes looked straight at Grace but before he had chance to say anything George spoke. "Yes that's right, you do have a traitor in your midst and it is not Dragon Brown."

Dragon Brown followed the conversation, thinking to himself that he had misjudged these little ones. They were not only unafraid but were willing to tackle Dragon Black head on. But who were they saying was a traitor?

Black reared up, snorted again this time bellowing black puffs of smoke out of his large nostrils. "So" he said, "who is the traitor if not Dragon Brown."

All four children in unison turned to their left where Dragon Green stood, and pointed. "He is your traitor!" they cried.

"Yes and his plans are to overthrow you," Grace added.

Black's head turned swiftly and his eyes darted towards Dragon Green, who was taken aback at the onslaught. "Don't believe a word they say," Green choked, spluttered and continued, "they are crafty liars and you don't have to take just my word. Dragon Yellow claims he was attacked by these four and remember," Green paused, then snarling at the five accused, bellowed "and it was Yellow who saw the fleeing army, not me. So don't call me the liar here, it is you lot!"

Green was feeling quite pleased with himself his manipulation of events were paying off and the outburst from the children seemed to reinforce his interrogation report now, being carefully studied once again by Dragon Black.

Black lifted his head and donning a large black leather cap tinged with white fur, swiped his tail back and forth three times, making noisy cracking sounds as it whipped through the air. "Enough" he said, "I am convinced of all your guilt and sentence you to immediate death by burning. You will be taken and thrown one by one into the volcano and let this be a lesson to any who try to overthrow me."

## Chapter 17

# The Race is On

Dragons, Blue, White, Pink and Gold were joined by Dragon Red who had been called to take them all in his fire truck. There was insufficient room for Yellow who was told to make his own way and join them, on reaching Volcano Peak.

"Can't we go any faster Dragon Red?" sighed a frustrated Dragon Pink. "If we don't get a move on it will be too late." Pink was riding in the cab with Dragon Red who, switching on the siren, placed his foot hard on the speed pedal. "I cannot go any faster we have too much weight on and it is an uphill climb."

On either side of the truck, Dragons Blue and Gold were hanging on for their lives. Each had one claw holding the gleaming brass rail and using their other claws were clutching onto a very frightened and worried Dragon White. All three dragons were propelled high into the air with every bump in the uneven track, before crashing back with a jolt.

The Dragon Council guards had now unlocked the chains securing the five prisoners to their individual granite rocks where they had stood and been sentenced to death. Each one was bound with more chains, making it absolutely impossible for them to escape and at best, for them to walk very slowly. They were being prodded and pushed towards the plinth's edge that slightly protruded over the circular mouth of the volcano.

Smoke, interspersed by the occasional flame drifted into the late morning sky, with the eerie silence broken only by the sound of the clinking chains being dragged across granite as each neared the edge and their final execution point. George and Grace glanced at the other two who were trembling, looking very scared and understandably worried.

"Don't worry" Grace said, putting on a brave face. "I am sure we will all get out of this."

Somewhat quietly for only Grace to hear, George was heard to say, "I really hope so, because time is really running out."

Dragon Brown had been thinking of ways to escape. He was being pushed more violently than the others, by one of the dragon guards. With a sudden movement, Brown caught the guard with one of his chains, wrapping it round the guard's right leg. The guard, caught unawares, tumbled over. But because he was linked by a short chain to Dragon Brown, he pulled him over as well.

Both dragons toppled head over tails until they finally stopped against a high rock that had until now obscured the track leading down to the town. Brown, unable to escape, saw out of the corner of his eye a red truck hurtling towards Volcano Peak with flashing lights. But it was too far away to hear the deafening siren.

Brown was approached by Green and the second guard and pulled violently to his chained feet. "There is no escape for you Brown," Green sneered. "Get him back to the others."

Brown was dragged towards where each of the children were standing on the very edges of their execution plinths, just a few centimetres away from certain death.

Grace felt the hot smoke and flames on her cheeks, the acrid fumes making her gasp for clean air as she coughed. She looked at her two brothers, who by her side, stood in front of their own execution plinth and looked on in horror.

Dragon Black had ordered that George be executed first and as he stood on his ledge, one dragon guard and Dragon Green approached each aside of Brown. "You stand there Brown" Green gestured to an empty plinth opposite George.

Brown moved as instructed, just as Green was about to push George to certain death. But before Green could touch him, Brown had whipped round, pulling his attached guard with him, making the guards tail flick round colliding with Dragon Green's large rear.

Green, was for an instant motionless, his eyes wide open as he started to lose balance, then with an almighty fearfully screeching yelp, the last he was ever going to make, Dragon Green toppled into the mouth of the volcano. There was finally a chilling scream followed by a short hushed silence immediately broken by the sound of the hurtling fire engine's siren, as it skidded to a halt, carrying the late would be rescuers.

## Chapter 18

# The Law Prevails

In all the kafuffle Dragon Black had not heard or seen the five dragons speed in until he had heard the siren that followed Green's desperate screams. Following at a breathless pace soon after was Dragon Yellow. Dragon Blue had dismounted the red carrier and presented himself in front of Dragon Black. "Sir," Blue started, "You are under arrest."

Dragon Black pulled himself to his full height, smiled, and in a threatening voice said: "Dragon Blue, be careful what you say. I am in no mood for frivolities. I urge you all to leave now whilst I am feeling benevolent." Black paused then menacingly lowered his head, his bad breath making Dragon Blue's eyes water, continued, "We do have plenty more room in the volcano for you all."

Dragon Gold sidled up to Dragon Blue. He had had enough. "Dragon Blue, continue to read out the charges, charges that I have endorsed and approved. The days of you continuing to rule by fear, Dragon Black, are over."

Black roared. "And who is going to attempt to apprehend me? Who has the courage to stand in my way?" Dragon Black looked towards the Draegonian Guards who were by now looking at each other in some confusion.

"They are not going to assist you, Black," Growled Dragon Gold. "As Mayor of Draegonia, under martial law, the state of emergency laws you yourself passed, I have the sole right to appoint a Commander in Chief. That commander…" Gold turned and looked straight towards Dragon Brown, who released from his chains, was helping the four children, "is Dragon Brown, he now commands the Draegonian Guard". Gold paused for breath then turning to Dragon Blue said, "Dragon Blue do your duty."

Dragon Blue stepped forward and as he did so Dragon Black made a move to flick his enormous and dangerous tail. But it did not move. Zach, during the arguments, had sneaked up behind the lofty stand Dragon Black was standing on. Black's long tail was hanging down, its tip rolled in a loop on the gravel floor.

Zach had used the chains that had previously bound him, to wrap round Dragon Black's tail, securing the end to a large protruding boulder. Black was restrained, he could not move without causing to himself significant injuries and it was the youngest of all, who had achieved his containment.

Dragon Black, crouched on all fours, was unable to move his long tail, his movements were severely restricted, he was going nowhere.

Dragon Blue stepped back and looking up to Dragon Black read out the charges: "Dragon Black you are charged with the following crimes: Holding a Judicial Court without following due Draegonian procedure.

1) Allowing unverified evidence to be presented.
2) Not allowing for a Jury.
3) Not hearing all evidence from all parties.
4) Passing sentences without due Draegonian authority.
5) Using unlawful means to procure the death penalty.
6) Attempted murder."

And at this point Dragon Blue took a deep breath and in a very firm and loud voice said:

"AND SEVEN, MURDER."

Dragon Gold nodded profusely, thanked Dragon Blue. As for the very first time a subservient Dragon Black looked on, Dragon Gold adopted his rightful role as judge and confirmed the arrest. "Dragon Black, you will be chained and taken from this place to a secure area within the Hall of Dragons where you will wait for your trial date to be confirmed. In the meantime the four children are to be given every kindness and support. They have been through an ordeal and if it had not been for Dragon Brown I fear George would have met an untimely death. Dragon Pink you are given the responsibility to take good care of them." Gold continued "Dragon Brown I want you to ensure that Dragon Black has a 24-hour guard and that Dragon Yellow is put under witness protection now that Dragon Green is dead. Yellow will be an important witness in this case. I am sure that the full process of law will prevail and that the sentencing of Dragon Black will rid us of all his evil."

The Draegonian Guards, first releasing Dragon Black's tail, unceremoniously dragged him down. Heavy restraining chains were firmly affixed to his legs. Dragon Black's tail was then chained under his body to prevent any deadly movement. Brown commanded them to ensure all chains were tight enough to prevent Black escaping but still enabling him to walk. The two Guards took positions front and rear of Dragon Black. In front of the procession was Dragon Blue with Dragon Yellow. He was now in protective custody. Following up the rear were Dragons White and Brown.

The secret entrance that Black had used to go back and forth from Volcano Peak to the Hall of Dragons was used by Black for the last time. The convoy using the entrance from the volcano leading into the labyrinth of tunnels marched Black to his holding point, where he would await trial.

The fire truck, this time with no siren or flashing lights descended in the midday sun towards the town of Draegonia. Now the cab held Dragons Gold and Red with Dragon pink ensuring that the four children, laughing, chatting and clinging to the side rails, were looked after. Their well being was now her responsibility.

## Chapter 19

# Finding an Antidote

Dragon Red stopped outside Dragon Pink's cave and the four children with Pink, alighted and entered her home. Pink was very tidy, everything in its place. Although Dragon Pink was small, the rooms of her cave were numerous and she did not hesitate in offering separate bedrooms for the four.

Zach and Joel wanted to share. Although brothers and usually wanting their own space, recent events had brought them very much closer together. Grace and George had rooms that would take any sized dragon. The ceilings of both rooms were high and illuminated by phosphorescence strips that lined the hard rock.

Pink realised that all the children had softer skins than dragons and would not be comfortable sleeping on the usual hard rock beds. She gave to each of them pillows she usually used to place her head on for a good night's sleep. These were to be the children's mattresses.

Joel could not contain himself any longer. "Where is the food" he cried? He had not eaten since they were captured by Dragon Green and his stomach was making weird gurgling sounds that made the others chuckle with embarrassment. Pink smiled a grin that made the children feel warm and safe. "I'll make you some dragon stew" she said and returned to the front of her cave where her kitchen was located.

George huddled the group together. "Look we need to think about how we are going to get home. We have been on this island for what appears to be an eternity." George was cut short by Grace, "It has only been three or is it four days," she said, counting the days out on her fingers.

"Irrespective how long we have been here," George continued, "We must find a way to get home." That evening all four ate a hearty meal and slept like logs, dreaming of finding a way back.

"Another day," Dragon Gold chanted to Dragon Blue as he arrived early to discuss the pending trial of Dragon Black. Removing an evidence container from his desk drawer, Blue stretched out his paw-like hand. He said: "I have spent most of the night finalising this for you. I have reviewed all the past open cases of missing dragons and believe that Dragon Black is behind them all. In addition I have re drafted the charge sheet to show the key crimes that we should concentrate upon."

Gold opened the container and peered in. "Well done, Dragon Blue. The sooner we deal with Dragon Black the better for all and looking at these charges I believe Dragon Black now faces the death penalty."

Blue nodded his head and showed Dragon Gold to the door. "So when will you convene the court hearing? I need to know in order to ensure all witnesses will be available and that their testimonies are fully prepared and checked." Blue looked at Gold for a reply.

"The day after tomorrow is good for me Blue, will you be ready?" Blue nodded, "Yes, no problem, the day after tomorrow it is then. I will post the times on the notice board outside if you issue the various individual notifications." Blue waved a half-hearted salute to Gold as Gold turned and departed to his chambers. He had a great deal of work to do.

Having had a good dragon breakfast of fried turnips and turtle eggs, washed down with dragon's orange juice and milk (Zach only drank milk) the four guests of Dragon Pink went to visit Dragon Blue, who they saw pinning an official notification to the notice board outside the station. Grace read it out aloud.

***Draegonia Notification of Hearing***

***The Council of Dragons hereby decree that Dragon Black will be tried at 10 Dragon Hours on the 164***

*Dragon Day for crimes against Dragons and Draegonia. Crimes include;*

1) *Attempted murder of Dragon Brown.*
2) *Attempted murder of George Slayer.*
3) *Attempted murder of Grace Garond.*
4) *Attempted murder of Joel Garond.*
5) *Attempted Murder of Zach Garond.*
6) *Aiding and abetting the death of Dragon Green.*
7) *172 cases of suspected murder in the first 'Dragon Degree'.*

*Signed:* *Dragon Blue*
*Chief of Draegonia Police*

"Whew," Joel exclaimed, "He's a real bad 'un!"

Zach re-reading the notice pointed to the last entry, "172 suspected murders. How has he managed to get away with it for so long?"

Dragon Blue overheard the remark and explained to the four that Dragon Black had until recently been a formidable creature. Being the only dragon that did not have clipped wings, he used to fly over the island on a regular basis, making all other dragons do his work and removing those who did not do his bidding. Dragon Blue further explained that over the years Dragon Black had became less willing to do anything for himself and just used fear and force to get his own way. However, sitting around all day on his throne and not getting any exercise had resulted in Dragon Black being somewhat out of his past and frighteningly fit condition. This together with the important fact that Dragon Black also had 'Flame Out' and therefore had lost his most powerful weapon had made his capture and restraint more possible.

"Grace, will we be at Dragon Black's trial?" Joel asked.

"Yes, I expect so. Is that right Dragon Blue?" she asked.

Dragon Blue, with a rather sterner face, nodded and with some sense of urgency, (he had been working for nearly 36 'Dragon Hours' now with very little sleep) informed them all that they would be called as witnesses and that they too would have to provide statements. Blue looked at his large 'Dragon Watch' suspended from a gold chain that he pulled from his chest pocket.

"There's no time like the present, come in and we will get them done straight away," he said. The children followed him through the door with it closing behind them - they would be busy for most of the day.

That evening Dragons Pink and White had met with the four children to have dinner. Dragon Chez

Rainbow was just one of three restaurants that were considered by Dragon Gold as outstanding and it was on his recommendation that the six had booked a table.

The cavernous room was decked with different coloured stone slabs placed centrally on cylinders of similar but contrasting coloured rock, allowing dragon legs to comfortably fit under the makeshift table tops. Dragons usually sit on their haunches, so no chairs could be seen.

The dragon restaurant's French Head Waiter appeared and greeted them. He was a multicoloured dragon that fitted in with the restaurant's name. He wore a small waistcoat with buttons made of special gem stones that glittered in the subdued light. "Table fer seex" he said, "thees-ah way."

They were all shown to a dragon table situated in the VID area (Very Important Dragons) close to a quartet that was providing music. One was on 'Dragon Drums', one on 'Dragon Guitar', one on 'Dragon Piano' the fourth was a singing female dragon. The mauve drummer was old and had grey stubble hair protruding from a narrow face with large bulbous eyes flickering from side to side as he kept beat with the music. The tangerine guitarist was not much taller but a great deal fatter. Working in clubs and drinking 'Dragon Brew' for years had given him a fat belly. He strummed lazily at the stringed instrument, tapping his foot in time with the music and looking bored with the whole thing.

The very dark beige pianist with a multi colour sash worn across his slim body, was a younger more energetic dragon, who every so often wanted to display his full talents by improvising and playing what appeared to be an entirely different tune, much to the confusion of the orange singer who would turn and gesticulate in a very unfriendly way to attract his attention, which abruptly brought him back to the original melody. As background music it was bearable but as a comic turn it was hilarious and made all four children roar with laughter at the antics.

The four children waited by the table as the Head Waiter sourced items for the children to sit on and bring them up to the height necessary to reach strange looking utensils that replaced their familiar knives and forks. George's and Grace's chairs were made of bamboo canes tied together with vine and shaped as a cube with a high back. Placed on the seat were brightly coloured sacks containing soft sponges taken from the sea.

"Wow, these are comfortable George." Grace said, hopping on to her recently made chair. Another cane made box was brought up for the remaining two boys. This time instead of a seat made for one it formed a bench for two, but the cushions were individually shaped to fit small bottoms.

Menus were handed to each dinner guest as another dragon sporting a white dinner jacket came across to pour water into cups made out of large coconut shells. Dragon White looked at the menu and recommended a starter of Pineapple and Salmon chunks on a bed of grass followed by Turtle Soup. For the main course White again pointed to the menu and exclaimed: "Oh, they have 'Tortoise Shell Supreme with Baked Rat'. Delicious!"

All four children cried out "Aghhh that sounds horrible!" Zach winced at the thought and Joel just yelled "I am definitely not eating that!!"

Dragon Pink laughed out loudly, "Dragon White is of course only joking, the Pineapple and Salmon starter is very tasty and especially for you the Dragon Chef has been requested to make you fish and those things you call potatoes all heated up in a special dragon fat." She continued: "We may not eat that type of food but know you'll like it." Four, very relieved and very hungry children settled back for a very strange, but delicious meal.

The meal was also consumed with vigorous conversation, each of the children asking in turn questions relating to where the dragons originally came from, why they had not left the island and eventually the chatter focussed on the problem of 'Flame Outs'.

All of a sudden Grace pointed her finger at Dragon White. "Is it the light in here or are those black spots fading?" she cried. George turned and looked at all the other dragons that, when they first entered the dimly lit restaurant, had the familiar 'telltale' black marks apparently caused by the virus spread by Dragon White.

Joel and Zach jumped down from their seat and ran out of the restaurant soon to return with some strange facts. "The dragons walking up and down outside still have the black spots and they do not appear to be fading," they cried.

"Sit down and don't leave the table unless told to do so or at least ask for permission next time, which was so bad mannered of you." Grace was not happy with the boys.

"Oh don't have ago at them, they are just trying to help." George was looking round as he spoke to see the reason why all the black spots on the dragons had faded to a light grey and on some were now disappearing altogether. "Are you certain you two that those outside still have their black spot infection?" Both boys answered in unison with an emphatic "Yes."

Dragon White and Pink looked bewildered. White asked if it could be the water and Pink offered the explanation as something in the food. George pondered and said he was sure that it was not to do with the water as it was supplied from the same source that every Dragon used. He was also sure it had nothing to do with the food as a quick look round at the different eating areas showed different foods being consumed. No, it had to be something else.

Then it dawned on him. High into the ceiling providing the illumination making all white and yellow things glow significantly whiter was a bluish glow that gave him the clue. "Grace," he whispered, "do you remember when we were down at our Nana's and Papa's villa in France last year we went to a restaurant where they used blue fluorescents lights as a means of sterilisation, you know killing insects such as mosquitoes?"

Grace nodded, and peering up to where the glowing strips were irradiating their light, said "That's it. That's the cure for the black spot virus - a good dose of being exposed to Ultra Violet Light!"

George explained to Dragon White their findings and that the restaurant had some form of chemical anomaly that turned the special lighting they had into UV. Grace suggested that both dragons should inform Dragon Gold to have every black spotted dragon pass through the restaurant, spending as much time under the light until their spots were all gone.

"This is good news," Pink spoke softly. "Everyone will be well pleased with you four and ……" she was interrupted by White, "Will it cure our 'Flame Out' George?" Before George could answer Grace piped up. "No I don't think the two problems are related. Clearly the spots are a virus and resulted from you sneezing over everyone spreading your germs. It shows you how important it is to wash your hands regularly and cough or sneeze into a hankie."

"A Hankie?" White exclaimed.

"Look" George interrupted, "if you organise the curing of the black spot as we suggest, we will try to find a way to re-ignite your flames. After all, if it was the flare from our safety pistol that caused the problem in the first place, we might be able to utilise it with some modifications to restore a flame in one dragon hot enough to ignite others."

Grace looked at George, he was her hero. Zach said he had a plan and Joel said he had an idea. "OK every one let's go," George said rising from the 'Dragon Table'. "We will go back to Dragon Pink's to start work on the Flame Out cure. White, you and Pink get to Dragon Gold and organise with him the communication process and timings for the black spot cure." The Head Waiter thinking there was something wrong with all the commotion was reassured by having the bill paid before all six finally left to put things right for Draegonia.

## Chapter 20

# A Cure for Black Spot & Flame Out

Dragon Red was outside the Dragon Fire Station as the children approached. Pink had used the 'Dragon Phone' in the restaurant before leaving and had asked Red to assist, if requested.

The three boys had discussed what they would need and had a mental list of materials and tools to achieve their plan. Picking up an assortment of items from Dragon Red's maintenance shed, they returned to Dragon Pink's dwelling.

In one of the many spare rooms of Dragon Pink's home, one proved ideal for a temporary work shop. All four realised the urgency of restoring dragon flames, as these were absolutely necessary for dragons to survive.

The ability to shoot flame was not only a defence mechanism but also used to heat stones for those cold winter nights, create fire for dragon furnaces and of course catch food on land, in the air or in water. 'Dragon Flame' was a matter of survival or extinction.

Working late into the night their plan was to cut down one of the three remaining ballistic charges used to fire the Vary Pistol, the gun that had caught Dragon White by surprise several days earlier.

"Look," said Joel working out the maths, "we need to reduce the explosive by at least a third if we are to prevent blowing off a dragon's head. We may have been fortunate in not killing Dragon White as the charge was fired from quite a distance, but to be sure of hitting the target this time without risk of injury, we will have to be a great deal closer and therefore the explosive charge has to be reduced." Zach confirmed Joel's figures and had actually started the delicate task of cutting back the charge using a saw like tool that dragons used to cut their nails.

"Be very careful with that" George said with a worried look on his face. "If you generate too much heat whilst cutting through, it could ignite and blow us all up and for goodness sake, move the other cartridges out of the way." There were three cartridges remaining from the pack of four from the raft.

Grace suggested that to minimise the possibility of injury, a test firing should be made. An hour passed and the delicate cutting of the charge down to

2/3rds of its original size had been completed when Dragon Pink returned. “Is that what will return all ‘Dragon Flames’?” she asked.

Zach was the first to respond, “We just don’t know until we run a test.” “That’s right” George spoke with Grace in support. “We need a safe place to fire the gun with this size of charge in it. We will then know if the correct amount of heat can be generated and we have asked Dragon Red to suggest a firing test range.”

Pink smiled. “And where has he suggested you test it?” Joel, not wanting to be left out as he had been working hard on the project as well piped in, “He has suggested we use the Great Hall’s large fire grate and chimney and to measure from the blast of our shot the temperature the rocks get to. Grace and George have calculated that the temperatures need to get to at least 3,000C.” At that precise moment there was a bang at the door and outside with his truck was Dragon Red ready with the motor running to take the four to the Great Hall.

It did not take long to get there and in fact the children could have walked, but Dragon Red was concerned that the firing test may not go well, cause an injury or start a fire and he wanted to have his equipment on hand just in case.

Passing through the main entrance the five could hear groans and growls coming from one corridor and its makeshift temporary cell. Dragon Black was still annoyed, he was still threatening everyone but now being fed only on dragon bread and water his energy levels were waning. With his constant moaning going on in the background echoing through the chambers, the five moved on into the Great Hall.

"Over there," pointed Joel. "Wow, it's enormous" Grace retorted. George and Zach checked and counted the 22 large round rocks that dragons breathed upon to heat. They were black as coal but clearly did not burn like coal and so large and so heavy that none of the children could move any of them.

George gave instructions. "OK, I want Joel to pace out 20 steps and mark the spot. Grace you remove any items that are in the fire surround or close by that could catch fire. Zach you come with me and we shall load the charge."

Dragon Red looked on, his head moving side to side watching with interest and without comment. Then it was time. George stood on the spot, 20 Joel paces from the fire, with Dragon Red and the three children behind him. Red not liking loud noises had his paws covering his ears, whilst Grace held onto Zach's and Joel's hands.

"Ready?" George cried. "Yes," came back the reply. **"FIRE."**

George pulled the trigger but instead of a device being exploded out of a gun hitting the Great Hall fire stones and the heat generated making them glow, there was nothing. George pulled the firing mechanism back for a second go. Dragon Red repositioned his paws on his ears and Grace firmly held onto her two brothers.

**"FIRE."** George shouted for the second time but still nothing. Zach and Joel rushed forward grabbed the gun and removed the cartridge. "I think the explosive is wet, damp or just too old to fire" he said unscrewing the metal case from the upper cartridge that had been earlier cut down to size.

Joel peering over Zach's shoulders saw something. "Look!" he cried. "The powder that's supposed to ignite and propel the explosive charge is a sticky mess. No wonder it didn't work! I think it must have got damaged in the storm, even though it looked as though the packing was OK."

Grace shouted above the noise, as the Great Hall again was consumed with the growls and barks of Dragon Black. "We need to get back and check the other two cartridges and hope that at least one of them is good enough to do the job!" Zach and Joel handed the bits and gun back to George as he urged them to be quick. "Look we need to hurry and work on a solution or we could be too late."

"Too late for what," Grace retorted. She could not quite see why George was in such a hurry or what difference of a couple of days would make. George could see that the other two boys and Dragon Red were staring at him wanting an answer too.

George waited for another of Dragon Black's outbursts to subside and explained. "Look guys, I know that Dragon Black is a tyrant and probably deserves the worst but I cannot get my head round the fact that he may get the death penalty and," George took a deep breath, "and I for one don't wish to see anyone or any dragon thrown into the volcano and hear the screams we heard when Dragon Green went in."

Dragon Red on hearing George's explanation came closer and said: "I am not a lover of Dragon Black but do agree we have had too many deaths. But how will getting a remedy as you call it, to reignite 'Dragon Flames' prevent the death sentence?"

George shook his head, "I don't know but if we can find a way, before the trial is concluded and sentenced passed, to cure the 'Flame Out' problem, then I am sure we will have a bargaining power." George paused again, and then in an urgent tone made the three children understand the importance of Dragon Black's survival. "Dragon Pink has very small wings that were not clipped but she is too young and unable to fly, well for at least a couple of years." George continued. "No other dragon on the island can fly, that is with the exception of Dragon Black. If Dragon Black is sentenced to death and the sentence carried out, we will lose our one main hope of leaving the island." George did not wait for an answer but led them all back to where the red truck was parked and returned to their temporary workshop for a second go.

Dragon Red so impressed by the determination of the little ones, agreed he would stay with them and would be on hand for the second attempt at firing the charge. Two more hours had passed and the five were hurtling back to the Hall of Dragons with the third of four cartridges. This test was going to be crucial for it would determine if the plan would work and importantly finalise the size of the final attempt to restore 'Dragon Flames'. The number three cartridge had been reduced to 2/3rds of its original size. The ignition charge essential to propel the explosive had this time been double checked. It had been contaminated and it had been lumpy but Joel had carefully crushed all the lumps making a smooth fine powder again and had tightly repacked the base of the charge with the powder and hemp. Joel's mark was still to be seen on the floor, exactly 20 paces from the great fire place.

Dragon Red once again placed his paws over his ears and Grace held tightly to the hands of her two brothers. All faces showed the stress of the occasion.

Was it going to work? Would the explosive charge, be too little, or too great?

George took up his position. He outstretched his right arm holding the gun, took aim and as he shouted "FIRE!" there was an almighty flash followed by an ear piercing screech as the ballistic cartridge containing its explosive charge shot across the room into the fireplace and with a deafening roar exploded. What followed next was both frightening and hilariously funny. The explosive detonated at the base, but in between the cracks of two of the largest boulders. There was a split-second pause and almost a slow motion effect as all 22 rocks propelled up the vast chimney were replaced by copious amounts of soot.

The fireplace was illuminated with reds, white, orange and blue flames causing immense heat. The thunderous noise and hot blasts of air knocked the children off their feet and as they picked themselves up they looked at Dragon Red who, covered in soot, was running for the fire extinguisher. Then there was silence.

However this did not last. A rumbling, a thudding and crashing could be heard as one by one the enormous boulders came crashing down into and across the Great Hall, all rolling in different directions. The four children had quickly turned on their heels and ran out of the Hall and peering back over their shoulders, they saw Dragon Red, skidding across the floor on his behind, having been bowled over by several of the round and very hot rocks.

Once again the children mounted the red truck and within a few minutes were joined by a very sooty Dragon Red who was vigorously brushing himself down.

"Come on everyone we must get back to work we only have one cartridge left to work with and definitely cannot make any mistakes next time." Grace replying to George's directive looked worried saying, "Do you really think we can take a chance using one of the dragons for the final charge based upon what we have just seen?"

Dragon Red interrupted, "Look of course I want us to get our flames back but really the risk is far too high to use that weapon of yours by firing it into one of our mouths. I for one would not volunteer." As the truck, with the children on board and deep in conversation, headed back to Dragon Pink's, the sky's blackness was starting to break as rays of light appeared from an early rising sun.

Once inside their makeshift workshop the children told Dragon Pink of their fraught attempt to get the balance right of having sufficient explosive and magnesium to create enough heat to re-ignite a dragons' flame. They told her that the first test failed because the powder required to project the missile was damaged, they explained that the second test actually went very well but proved that if the shot exploded in such a small confined place as a dragon's mouth, it would or could be fatal.

"I have an idea." It was Zach who spoke. "Why not remove as much of the powder so that the speed of the missile is substantially reduced and remove more of the explosive?"

George thought for a moment, "Ummm, I am not sure" he said, "the charge needs speed to detonate the explosive and if it does not detonate, it would be useless. And" he continued, "If we reduce the powder content that actually fires the projectile then it may also alter the accuracy of hitting the precise target."

"I can sort that out" piped in Joel, "All we have to do is put an extension tube on the muzzle of the gun. Making it longer will help to keep the explosive charge projection with greater accuracy."

"You know" Grace interjected, "that's a great idea Joel and I have an idea regarding the amount of explosive needed and how it can be used."

The three boys all looked at Grace quizzically, waiting for her to explain further. "Look" she said picking up the remaining complete charge, "we are trying to reduce the amount of powder necessary to fire the projectile but still make it explode by detonation through impact. This is still going to increase the explosion at considerable risk to those closes by." She continued: "What if we reduce the ignition powder and the explosive charge down to one third in other words half of what we used in our last test."

George, shaking his head, informed them all it wouldn't work. "You see," he said, "reducing the speed or, using its technical term, the velocity..." They all raised their eyebrows. This was not the time for talking too technical. "Keep it simple George" said Grace with a smile. "OK, if the speed is reduced there will be insufficient force of impact to detonate the charge."

"But George" Grace retorted, "There is another way to detonate. We can use fire." The other three children laughed with Joel speaking out aloud, "I suppose you're saying we should first light a fire in a dragon's mouth and fire the charge into it. But that wouldn't work as a small fire would not generate sufficient heat and anyway it would be very uncomfortable for any volunteering dragon."

"I could do it," Dragon Pink had been looking on and listening with interest, she continued in a very calm and decisive voice. "I am the only dragon on Draegonia that still has 'Dragon Flame'. I know it is not hot enough to ignite other dragon flames, as you know I have tried with several, BUT my small flame would definitely ignite any explosive charge.

The four children first looked at each other, this solution had not crossed their minds. The plan was still untried and known to be dangerous and Dragon Pink was their true friend they did not wish to hurt. After some discussion they all agreed the risk was too great. “We don’t know if one third of the charge would be good enough to make your flame hot enough to ignite others,” said George. Zach in a more worried tone said, “We don’t want to put your life at risk.” Joel just stood quietly, thinking of the harm another failed attempt would cause. Before Grace had any time to make her opinion known, Pink in a rather loud voice for her, spoke. “Enough, I have every confidence in you, I know that you will do nothing to deliberately harm me and that you will take every care. But without ‘Dragon Flame’ all dragons on Draegonia will eventually die, and I will not let that happen, without giving my all.”

The four did not argue, but with greater urgency set about making for the last time a device that with Dragon Pink’s brave involvement could well work and restore ‘Dragon Flames’.

## Chapter 21

# Dragon Black on Trial

Within the Great Hall there was much chatter as the time was fast approaching when Dragon Black would be brought from his cell and placed in the prisoner's dock. He would be anchored to the floor by chains to each of his hind legs and his wings strapped to prevent him from expanding them. His gigantic tail would also be tied to his back to prevent him from whipping those nearby. Dragon Black's throne had now been converted to a judge's bench, where Dragon Gold in all his splendour would take charge of proceedings supported either side by legal advisors.

In front of him were two separate blocks, each supported on either side by two rectangular plinths. Standing behind these, to the right, was Dragon Mauve for the prosecution and on the left Dragon Purple for the defence. Both Mauve and Purple sported the customary legal silk gowns. High on both sides of the hall were two spectator galleries, full to capacity with dragons, who had scores to settle with Black and were delighted at his predicament.

A hush settled over the Hall as Dragon Onyx, the clerk to the court entered. He stood immediately under where Dragon Gold would preside and in an emphatic legal voice proclaimed: "Be all upstanding for the Judge. The court is in session Draegonia vs. Dragon Black." As Onyx spoke the doors at the rear of the hall opened and in walked Dragon Gold with his legal advisors who took up their places. "All be seated" Onyx ordered. All dragons including those in the gallery sat down, many started to chat noisily. Onyx, without looking to where the chatter was coming from was heard to cry "Silence in the Court" and if one had dropped you could have heard a 'Dragon Pin'.

The Clerk of the Court then picked up his charge sheet, prepared by the 'Draegonian Prosecution', instructed Dragon Black to rise and then read out the crimes and charges made against him. On completion, Onyx looked squarely at Dragon Black and asked "How do you plead, Guilty or Not Guilty?"

Unsurprisingly Dragon Black just growled: "Not guilty of all charges." He was then told to sit down as Dragon Mauve stood up and presented the case for the prosecution. The trial was now in full swing.

Meanwhile inside the makeshift workshop the four children had been working furiously to change the barrel of the Flare Gun and to modify the last remaining cartridge. It was once more necessary to remove the cartridge's lumpy ignition powder and grind it down to a fine black dust. Joel then weighed it and removed 60%, mixing the remainder with some hemp and tightly packing it into the base of the shell.

Zach had been busy cutting the explosive charge down to a third of its original size. Grace placed the remaining two thirds with that left over from the previous failed test in one of Dragon Pink's smaller wooden chests, for safe keeping.

George supervised, clearing away the mess caused by so much activity. Both the gun and cartridge had been modified, they were ready. It was lunchtime and everyone, especially Joel, was very hungry. They had only had a snack at breakfast and now their stomachs were making gurgling noises.

Dragon Pink brought in some coconut milk, fresh orange juice and cold water on a tray that also had two plates of 'Dragon Sandwiches' containing an assortment of fillings. "You must eat," she said placing the tray on the bench table, moving tools and old cartridge casings. "Be careful" Joel exclaimed. "We don't want to lose anything, you never know if these will be needed again."

Dragon Pink was only interested in feeding the four, she smiled and asked what time would they be ready and where was the experiment to take place. "At the Dragon Hall about"...George looking at his watch paused. "Oh!" He exclaimed. "The court of course is in session and we cannot use it."

Grace responded. "George it does not matter where we do the deed so long as we have Dragon Red and perhaps a dragon doctor standing by, I do not want to take any chances."

Dragon Pink laughed, "You're worrying too much and anyway apart from Dragon Red, who has agreed to help, all other dragons are cramped up in the Great Hall listening to the case against Dragon Black. In fact, I believe the defence is so weak that sentencing could well be given this afternoon."

"Well that's it." George hurriedly said."Zach, you go and alert Dragon Red we are ready and that we will carry out the firing outside the Fire Station." Looking at Dragon Pink, and in a softer voice, George asked. "Are you ready, Pink?" Pink just nodded and moved towards the door. "Let's get it over with." She said.

The four joined Zach and the Fire Chief outside his premises where he had cordoned off a section. Although all other dragons were busy elsewhere, he was not going to take any chances. "Is this going to work?" he said looking hard at George and Grace. "I don't much care for the idea of you shooting into Dragon Pink those explosives especially after last night's fiasco."

The children did not speak. They were also worried, but now was not the time to voice their real concerns for Dragon Pink's safety.

## Chapter 22

# Justice

Back at the Great Hall the day had been gruelling for Black. He was made to listen to all his alleged crimes as one by one witnesses came forward to give their account of Black's involvement in the disappearance of their relatives or friends. Dragon Black just scowled and through his defence argued that no one had actually witnessed any deaths and it was shear speculation that he, Dragon Black, had murdered any of them.

The prosecution counter argued that it was not a Draegonian legal point to present a body and that it was a fact that the last dragon to see all of the 172 missing ones was in fact Dragon Black and that this could not just be coincidence. Dragon Black looked on, murmuring that he would get even, as charges, accusations and counter arguments were tossed from prosecution to defence and back.

The court had adjourned for lunch and had returned to hear final arguments and the findings that were to be summed up by Dragon Gold, The Judge.

Draegonian legal system (in this case) did not call for a jury and relied solely on the findings of the presiding judge. Once sentence was passed there was no right of appeal and Black looked on in horror as he knew his time was almost up. Black was told by Onyx to stand.

Dragon Gold spoke; there was a hush throughout the court;

"*This is a complex case in part, yet has some components that are very straightforward to deal with and I shall focus on these first.*

*The Charges brought against you Dragon Black have been well argued by your defence and you have been given every opportunity to put your views across. I shall now deal with the charges made against you one by one.*

1) ***The Attempted Murder of Dragon Brown.***

   *The evidence is overwhelming and has been proved conclusively that you did with intent use your powers and the Draegonia legal system to falsify evidence in collusion with Dragon Green to falsely pass a death sentence on Dragon Brown. To this charge I find you guilty and sentence you to 10 Years Hard Labour.*

2) ***The Attempted Murder of George Slayer.***

*The facts have been evaluated and it is unclear as to whether or not you were in league or not in league with Dragon Green, specifically in the attempted murder plot. But the court does find you Guilty of perverting Dragon justice and believe that you failed deliberately to take every opportunity to allow him to prove his innocence. Thus on this account I do find you GUILTY and sentence you to a further 10 Years Hard labour.*

3) ***The Attempted Murder of Grace Garond.***
4) ***The Attempted Murder of Joel Garond.***
5) ***The Attempted Murder of Zach Garond.***

*On these three accounts my findings are no different from those surrounding George Slayer. It is fortunate that visitors to our island did not die and I treat this matter with the seriousness it deserves.*

Dragon Judge Gold was just about to pass another sentence when there was a loud gun fire, a scream and ear piercing screech, then silence. Everyone in the court room started to ask and discuss what the noise was, where it was coming from and who had caused it? Unknown to them all George had fired the last of the home made explosive devices straight into the mouth of Dragon Pink, the screams were hers.

Dragon Onyx, clearing his throat shouted twice, "Silence in The Court." The second much louder shout brought immediate silence and Judge Gold continued his summing up and sentencing.

*"As I said before the interruption, I treat these offences with the seriousness they deserve and sentence you Dragon Black to a further Thirty Years Hard Labour.*

*Now to Charge 6.*

***The Aiding and abetting the death of Dragon Green.***

*Dragon Green's death I believe was more of his own making and as a key player in the intrigue of a fictitious invading force, the cohersion and persuasion of Dragon Yellow to lie, I feel met an untimely death that I will record as misadventure. In doing so Dragon Black I cannot find you Guilty of his death, thus on this charge, I find you* **NOT GUILTY."**

There was a loud exclamation from the audience of on looking dragons who expected at least a guilty sentence and a greater expectation that Black would have faced the death penalty.

"Quiet in the Court," Onyx called once more.

Judge Dragon Gold again paused, looked at Dragon Black and this time the Judge's face twitched as he held back some considerable anger.

"*I will now move onto the more serious charge that I tell the court and especially you Dragon Black that carries an automatic death penalty. I refer to the charge of:*

***172 cases of suspected murder in the First Degree***

The court was so silent that as the Judge clearly spoke you could hear his voice echoing throughout the chambers.

"*Dragon Black we have heard witness after witness implicate you in the disappearances of 172 dragons over the past one thousand Dragon Years. I have heard all the evidence.*"

Pausing for breath Dragon Judge Gold stretched out his claws, pulled from beneath his table top a black cap and placed it upon his judicial head.

The entire court knew that this was the moment. Dragon Black was about to be sentenced to death.

## Chapter 23

# Intervention

George took aim, Dragon Pink stood twenty Joel paces from where she was about to receive a missile, fired from the extended barrel of a gun, now held and ready to fire in the hands of George.

"Good luck," said Dragon Red, hardly bearing to look with his paws held tightly protecting his ears. Dragon Pink opened her dainty little mouth, this time with no smile. She shut her eyes and braced herself. Grace instructed her to take a deep breath and blow a flame out of her mouth and that would indicate to George she was ready. It was also necessary for her flames to be strong and hot enough to ignite the incoming explosive charge.

"I'm ready," she nervously said and with that took a deep breath and spat a white hot fire streak from her open mouth. George instantaneously squeezed the trigger and fired the projectile in a thunderous bang. The missile entered Dragon Pink's mouth with her white hot breath exploding the reduced charge, but still knocking her off balance with such force, she let out a mighty screech.

There was a minute that seemed an eternity of silence. Dragon Pink's eyes were spinning counter clock wise as she staggered to her feet. Dragon Red and the children rushed to her aid but before they could reach her she bellowed out a roar and with it out shot flames several feet high of reds, oranges, and blues. Her Dragon Flame was even stronger than Dragon Black's had been in the past.

"Quick" said Grace, "try to ignite Dragon Red's flame!" Dragon Red opened his mouth and Pink fired into it a terrific red and blue flame that gave off tremendous heat. Immediately Dragon Red's Flame was restored... **A Success**.

The three boys cheered. Grace hugged Dragon Pink with affection, "Well done," she said, as Dragon Red was opening and closing his mouth, exercising his restored flame.

George looking at his watch exclaimed. "Quick, we have no time to lose. If they sentence Black to death we will lose what chance we have of getting off this island." Dragon Red led the four racing towards the Hall of Dragons, closely followed by Dragon Pink.

It was both Grace and George who reached the main entrance first. They had run their hearts out and on entering the Court Room spied Dragon Judge Gold placing a black cap on his head, just about to pass sentence of death. The two, in one voice shouted out as loud as they could "WAIT, WE HAVE IMPORTANT INFORMATION!"

Every dragon turned their heads, some stretching to see the two children and the others now appearing in the court room behind them. Dragon Onyx was not amused. He shouted the familiar "Silence in court," but this time no one took any notice.

Judge Gold banged on his desk furiously "Order, Order. Order!" he demanded. Gradually, silence returned. George stepped forward for all to hear. In a firm voice he said. "May I have your permission to address the court, Sir?" Dragon Judge Gold quite liked George and bending a rule that he would not have bent for anyone else, responded. "I will let you speak but if you waste the courts time, I will hold you in contempt, do you understand?" George moved closer still with his three companions joining his side. Once more, with supreme confidence, in a clear voice, he said.

"Sir, I see that we may be just in time to prevent you passing the death penalty on Dragon Black."

The galleries of dragons came alive with chatter, Dragon Black's ears pricked up, his glazed eyes becoming sharper, his jaw dropping. "What?"

demanded Dragon Judge Gold, "Do you really understand what you are saying? The conviction of 172 dragon murders must carry the deserved and ultimate penalty."

George stood his ground, "Sir, of course Dragon Black should be given the full penalty for the crimes he has committed, I cannot argue with that, but by killing Dragon Black you may well inadvertently kill us too." George pointed to each of his cousins. "You see Sir, Dragon Black is really the only one who can get us home. Kill him and we are left stranded and cannot survive on Draegonia for long. Dragons are unable to survive for too long without 'Dragon Flames' as are we unable to survive on Draegonia for any length of time."

There was an agreement by various nods of dragon heads to George's argument. "But Dragon Black has to face punishment for his crimes." Gold responded. "Or have you got a viable solution."

Grace interjected, "Sir let us inform you of some tremendous and welcome news. We have found an antidote for your 'Flame Outs' and Dragon Red here will confirm that we now have a cure." Dragon Red bellowed out a burst of flame that tore across the court room floor from his mouth. Dragon Pink laughed at this and in so doing also bellowed out huge bluish hot flames taking Dragon Onyx by such surprise he dropped all his notes. "That is indeed very good and most welcome news." Gold applauded, "how long will it take to cure every dragon?"

George laughed. "It will be far quicker if we start right away rather than waste valuable time in attending the death of this miserable creature and we have a plan for him that we believe you will approve of."

Dragon Judge Gold roared for silence and in a stern authoritative voice, his eyes piercing through Dragon Black, passed judgement. "You have thus far been sentenced to 50 years hard labour. This judgement will stand. You will be immediately taken to the north of the island under close guard where on bread and water you will serve time with hard labour and once we have reviewed further sentencing you will return for final judgement, take him down."

Dragon Black was unchained and escorted away by several guards. Gold adjourned the court and requested the children to meet with him and Dragon Brown in his chambers. He also ordered Dragons Pink and Red to start the re-ignition of all dragon flames.

## Chapter 24

# The Way Home

Dragon Gold entered the inner chamber situated within the Hall of Dragons. This room was very regal as it represented the highest legal rank of Draegonia, The Judge. One wall contained stone shelves of 'Dragon Reference Books'. On another wall were paintings of previous Judges dating back some hundreds of years. The paintings were not in frames of any kind but had been drawn and coloured straight onto the wall, leaving very little space for further additions.

Close to the third wall stood a large round table and of course no chairs. The table was made out of jet black granite that had been highly polished, the edges of which displayed many layers, indicating its very old age.

Dragon Brown and the four children now stood in front of Dragon Gold who had sat down on his haunches, his upper body straight and looking very severe spoke. "Now then, I am of course pleased and all Draegonia is indebted to you for the return of our flames." Dragon Brown nodded and made noises of agreement. Clearing his throat the Judge continued. "**Huh-herrr**, we do have a problem though and that is we must impose a sentence on Dragon Black that meets the severity of his crimes. The death penalty I am afraid is the ultimate price he must pay."

Joel sighed and looked very unhappy as Zach very pointedly spoke out. "So, what about us, we did nothing to harm you, we've been locked up, chained up, tried for crimes we have not committed, almost killed and yet still helped you lot?"

"Shush," exclaimed Grace, "don't be so rude to the Judge he is only explaining things as he sees it." Judge Gold smiled lowered his shoulders and whispered to Grace, "He's a fiery little chap isn't he?"

At this point George who had been preparing himself spoke up. "If we showed you a way whereby Draegonia Justice was seen to be done and that Dragon Black was given an appropriate sentence befitting his crimes" George paused, "would you consider a slightly amended form of punishment?"

Dragon Judge Gold pondered on these words. "I am not sure what you mean George. The problem as I see it is that Dragon Black has to be sentenced to death for the crimes he has committed."

George spoke quickly in reply, “Yes we know that but there is of course the factor of timing. Look, Draegonia law can still apply the death penalty but in a new form.”

“Explain” The Judge said looking at Dragon Brown who shrugged his shoulders, wondering what the four had cooked up.

“Well,” continued George, “dragons do not live very long without their ‘Dragon Flame’ do they?” George continued with both dragons listening intently to his every word. “The Court can still find Dragon Black Guilty of the murders and still sentence him to death, but use a different method than the throwing him into the Volcano.”

“Go on,” Dragon Gold gestured.

“You see Sir,” George continued, “you will still find Dragon Black Guilty and you will still sentence him to death but a far worse death than the quick death of the volcano. You will first banish Dragon Black from ever returning to Draegonia. Next you will stipulate that his ‘Dragon Flame’ will not be ignited, it will mean a sentence of slow death.”

Dragon Gold pondered on what he had heard and then asked. “But how does this help you?”

Grace piped up. “That’s easy. You command Dragon Black that he will serve a period of hard labour working an 18 hour day and being fed only on bread and water until he has shed enough weight to enable him to once more fly and carry us back home."

"I still do not see how this helps the four of you," Gold exclaimed, "especially if Dragon Black agrees but whilst flying you out of Draegonia drops you all from a great height to your own deaths."

"We've thought of that" it was Joel's turn to speak. "You see, we have enough explosive material left over from the charges we adapted to cure the 'Flame Outs' to make a special collar for Dragon Black. A collar that he would be unable to remove without a special electronic key that we will make using the hand held emergency radio we still have from the life raft."

Zach not to be out done with the exciting revelations interrupted. "And we can control Dragon Black by letting him know that we can detonate his collar using the transmitter within a 25 mile radius, so any slight hint that he was to double cross us..." Zach paused, smiled, outstretched his arms and bringing his hands together in an almighty clap shouted "BOOM, no more Dragon Black!"

Dragons Gold and Brown looked at each other and nodded. "The proposal is acceptable." Dragon Gold chanted thrashing his tail in a poor imitation of how Dragon Black used to do it. "But how long will it take for you to make the explosive collar and transmitting device?" Dragon Brown enquired.

George finalised everything and gained complete approval from Dragon Gold. It was agreed that Dragon Black would the very next day be brought back for sentencing. His 50 Years Hard Labour sentence would still apply but he would be informed that if he agreed to safely fly the four back to their homes, the 50 year Hard Labour sentence already imposed would be deferred or held over provided Dragon Black committed no more future crimes.

That very next day Black was in front of Dragon Judge Gold, listening to the conditions of his sentence. Black thought they were soft, had lost their senses, he certainly had no intentions of flying the kids back home. No, he was thinking how he could drop them from a great height and return to Draegonia and teach everyone a bitter lesson. His thoughts were broken by Dragon Gold dropping a bombshell on him.

"Yes Dragon Black," Gold coldly stated. "You may well think we are being soft." Dragon Black shook his head showing some false humility. "But," he continued. "You are definitely not to be trusted. Firstly, we are imposing a death penalty for your heinous crimes of murder. Volcanic death is too good for you and far too swift."

Dragon Black was not sure where all this was leading and with eyes narrowing, glared first at the children, who were high up in the Gallery, then at Dragon Gold who had placed upon his head the traditional death cap. "Dragon Black" the Judge said, "your flame will not and never will be re-ignited. You will suffer a painful death overtime associated with 'Flame Out'. You will be fitted with a special explosive device, the collar of which will be electronically locked around your neck."

The on-looking dragons gasped and murmurs reverberated around the Great Hall. "Silence in Court" Dragon Onyx shouted. Dragon Gold continued. "Furthermore, it is estimated that two weeks further hard labour, working 18 hours per day and fed only on bread and water will have you fit to fly."

More murmurs filtered into the silence broken only by Dragon Gold's sentencing voice. "Once you have lost that fat and become fitter to fly the banishment order will take effect. It is a condition of sentencing that you agree, without reservation, to return the four children back to their homes safely." Dragon Judge Gold stood up and with a dominant gesture and cold hard voice spoke directly to Dragon Black. "DO YOU AGREE TO SAFELY RETURN THE CHILDREN HOME AND ACCEPT THE TERMS OF YOUR SENTENCE?"

Dragon Black who was thinking furiously of a way out realised that if he did not agree then he would without any doubt, be sentenced to immediate death by Volcanic Action, a death he fervently wished to avoid.

Black moved his head from side to side, his steely eyes taking note of each of his accusers. A hush fell around the court as he spoke, his voice cold without feeling, dragons listening to his every word. "I still profess my innocence and will prove this to you all." Black was a cunning old and very devious dragon even at a time of facing death, "I of course will be pleased," he licked his lips and with grinding sounds of teeth gnashing together, continued "and it will be my pleasure to assist the children every way I can. I of course accept the judgement of the court." Dragon Gold thrashed his tail three times indicating the Court had made its final and binding judgement.

## CHAPTER 25

# Home at Last

The furthest most part of Draegonia, to the north, is rugged and bleak, facing usually rough seas. Dragon Black's sentence of hard labour sees him under tight guard, moving large boulders of heavy volcanic rock 200 metres into the sea. His task has been to form a breakwater that eventually will be joined either side to make a lagoon. He has sweated and toiled nonstop for 18 hours a day and the diet regime imposed on him, together with the hard work, has made him fitter, slimmer and even more formidable looking than when two weeks earlier he was sentenced.

As he moves the final block to complete the breakwater, Dragon Brown appears on the rocky shore line and Dragon Black wades back towards him. Dragon Black's legs and tail are still heavily chained. On approaching the water's edge Black overhears Dragon Brown informing the guards that Black is to be taken back to Draegonia Central where Dragon Red and Dragon Smokey Blue, Draegonia's Chief Technical Dragon, are waiting with George and the three other children for his arrival. Dragon Black thinks of how he can escape. His thoughts focus on how he will wreak revenge, how he will make everyone suffer and how he will deal with the four who have caused him so much humiliation and pain.

Black's thoughts are interrupted as he is dragon-handled, placed under heavy guard and unceremoniously marched to the awaiting crowd of dragons who now filled the main square. On arrival, to numerous jeers and growls from the crowd encircling him, Dragon Black is restrained by his guards during the fitting of a large iron collar around his neck. A loud click is heard, as George and Joel presses home and securely locks the collar. Grace holds a tiny black taped box with a small silver aerial protruding from it.

"The collar is a very tight fit, Grace. Dragon Black won't get out of that in a hurry." Grace looks up at George who helping Joel down from the ladder perched against Dragon Black's long neck, adds. "In fact we can honestly say it is made to measure." All four as well as Dragon Red, Pink and Smokey Blue roared with laughter. Dragon Black makes no move, all the while thinking his time will come.

Whilst Dragon Black had been in the north serving part of his Hard Labour sentence, the four children had also been hard at work. The iron rings of a washed up wine barrel had been forged using 'Dragon

Flame' and heat into a perfect fitting metal collar. The locking mechanism obtained from an old chest was packed with the explosive left over from the reduced sized cartridges of the flares that had been used to restore the 'Dragon Flame'. The three boys had worked together to modify the emergency radio into two units: one to act as a receiver and detonator and fitted within the collars explosive packed lock and the other to transmit the firing signal.

Now the day had come to put everything together. Black was fitted with his explosive collar and all the dragons had turned out to witness their departure from Draegonia. The children had been given a number of small gifts now packed in the bag that originally had held their survival equipment. Dragon Pink had organised several of her friends to make farewell banners and were now proudly displaying them. They read;

*Thank You for Restoring Our Flames.*
*Come back and see us sometime.*
*Remember us as your Dragon Friends*

And one held at one corner by Dragon Pink just had three words.

*We Love You*

Pink had tears in her eyes, "Please come back sometime to see us," she said.

Dragon Gold moved forward, his Gold Chain glistening in the mid afternoon sun. First he spoke to Dragon Black. “Dragon Black, you have completed just 14 days of your 50 Year Hard Labour Sentence, I am sure you do not wish to do anymore. You also have a collar filled with high explosive that should you try to do any foul deed between now and taking the children home, will result in detonation and your head being blown off.”

All the dragons surrounding Dragon Black laughed and as they did so flames spouted out of their mouths in all directions demonstrating that their flames had been fully restored.

Dragon Gold pointed to a specially designed four seat saddle arrangement and ordered it to be affixed to Dragon Black’s back. “Dragon Black” Gold spoke yet again in an authoritative manner. “You may well think that whilst the four children are seated on your back you could fly them anywhere other than their home and that they can’t do anything about it. Well” Gold continued, “the seat you see being fitted to your back also has a means of being detonated. It has been fitted with what the children call a parachute. The seat would serve as a boat over water but wherever and for whatever reason it should be used make no mistake, it allows the children to also detonate your collar, without them being harmed.”

Dragon Black said nothing. He had no idea how he would wreak revenge but knew this was not the time or place to show his hatred for them all. For now he would do as he was told, anything to get away.

The four children strapped themselves into their seats and as the dragons released the chains locked to Black's legs and tail he outstretched his wings and with a mighty flap lifted off the ground flying high into the air. He circled high above, looking down on what he now considered, were his deadly adversaries and with a final flap of his huge wings, shot off Westwards, into the setting Sun.

Darkness fell and as the black dragon approached the shores of England the four children felt a sense of relief. This had been an adventure they would all talk about to each other, but how would they explain things to their parents?

The thought of explaining about being lost in a storm, washed up on what they thought was a desert island only to learn it was full of coloured dragons and that they had been arrested sentenced to death, escaped and flown back home by a black dragon, was going to be difficult if not impossible.

Their chatter and thought sharing was interrupted as George pointed to where the two younger boys and Grace lived. Their house lights were still on as the black dragon carefully landed and allowed them off. "Bye George," the three all said together and waved, as once more Dragon Black soared into the night sky and finally headed For George's house. His Mum, who had waved George a good bye only that morning, was peering out of the window, just as the dragon landed. She rushed out exclaiming, "Where the.... have you been?" But then seeing the shadow of Dragon Black as he lifted off yet again into the night sky, passing over the house, she blinked and hugging George said. "This had better be a good story."

Meanwhile Dragon Black, still with the four seats and explosive collar strapped to him, headed eastwards, growling and spitting black puffs of smutty smoke from his flameless mouth ...

**"IF THEY THINK THIS IS THE END, WELL IT'S NOT!!**

# EPILOGUE

The Dragons of Draegonia carry a number of messages for all to learn from.

Operating as a team, the four children survive a number of ordeals. They work together. They look after each other and are bonded more by friendship than blood relationships.

Colours have a distinct bearing on how we perceive things, the language we use, people and attitude. Green is traditionally used in conjunction with 'Envy'. Yellow in relationship to cowardice, Pink all things nice and sweet the opposite to Black that often signifies the darker side of life.

The narrative follows those problems that can grow from exaggerations or untruths and unveils the lies that create the need for more lies. Children of all ages learn by example and the Dragons of Draegonia places their imaginations in the midst of the need to survive as a result of those telling lies to derive direct benefit and those exaggerating events to cover up perhaps their own inadequacies.

Simple lessons to be learnt;

1) Work Together especially when things are difficult.
2) Don't give up, just try harder.
3) Be supportive and see the best in others.
4) Don't be envious of others.
5) Cowardice is not respected.
6) Don't Bully or try to control through Fear.
7) Learn as much as you can whilst at school, you never know when the knowledge will be useful.
8) Communicate and discuss things rather than give up.
9) Abide by the law.

**And finally:**

10) Always inform your parents or guardians where you're going, for they will be worried if they do not know where you are.

# Glossary

**Book 1** — **Dragons of Draegonia**
**The Adventure Begins**

**Dragon Black** — The self appointed leader, the most scary and most feared dragon of all. Black is the largest of all dragons, uses his long steel like tail as both a lethal weapon and symbol of authority. Black sports two enormous powerful wings and is the only dragon that can fly. His threatening appearance is further enhanced by two fiery red piercing eyes. Dragon Black is one dragon never to be crossed.

**Dragon Gold** — The Mayor and Part Time Judge. Gold is a little pompous, full of his own self importance, a worrier, honest and absolutely fair. He waddles due to a rather fat stomach and little exercise.

**Dragon Blue** — Head of the Draegonia Dragon Police Force. He is a little on the plump side, stern faced and a stickler for implementing the law.

**Dragon Red** — Head of Draegonia's Fire Service. Dragon Red is very fit and has a good sense of humour. Red does not put fires out but starts them for those dragons that may have lost their flames.

**Dragon Brown** Recently appointed as Commander in Chief of the Draegonia Army. One of the oldest of dragons, he can be abrupt and austere Brown is astute, can be quick witted and respected.

**Dragon Green.** Disliked by many because of his envious nature and willing to do almost anything to get his own way, even if he has to lie. His eyes are very close together; his ears twitch a great deal, specifically being more pronounced when he tells lies.

**Dragon Yellow** As is his colour, he is yellow in nature frightened often of his own shadow. Tends to rush and bump into things especially when he has concerns or his anxiety level is raised.

**Dragon White** A large female dragon responsible for the environment of the South Island. She has a very large mouth and cleans the beach by turning drift wood into ashes with one burst of her ferocious flames.

**Dragon Cream** Sister to Dragon White who patrols the northern side of the Island also keeping it clear of washed up debris. Like her sister she also has the ability to shoot flames up to ten meters turning everything to dust and ashes in its path.

| | |
|---|---|
| **Dragon Rainbow** | Head waiter of the exclusive Draegonia Rainbow Restaurant. Originally from the South of France, Rainbow Dragon speaks with a very strong French accent. |
| **Dragon Pink** | The youngest and smallest of all dragons. She is the friendliest and kindest of all and is the only dragon (apart from Dragon Black) that has not had her wings clipped. She however is still too young to fly. Dragon Pink has important ancestry and is a direct descendent of a Wizard Dragon. |
| **Dragon Onyx** | Onyx is Clerk to the Draegonian Court. He has a distinctive and very loud autocratic voice and a head that never stays still for a moment. |
| **Dragon Smokey Blue** | Draegonia's Chief Technical Dragon. A scientist typified by his large monocle necessary for his weak right eye. Although very intelligent has a habit of staring but not finishing sentences, assuming those around him, have understood his point, without any further explanation. |
| **Dragon Mauve** | A self opinionated legal prosecutor who talks in legalise. He has long thin dragon paws that he uses to direct his audiences attention. |
| **Dragon Purple** | Dragon Purple is the court's appointed legal defender. He is a slick, smooth talking dragon able to twist witness statements to his advantage. Being |

| | |
|---|---|
| | shorter than Dragon Mauve he tends to roll back and forth on his hind legs, occasionally standing on the tips of his feet, to gain extra height. |
| **Dragon Grey** | Draegonia's Chief Physician. Dragons rarely become ill thus the Draegonia Hospital is mainly used as a dragon maternity unit and research centre. Grey's main duties are as 'Personal Physician' to Dragon Black who has made Grey responsible for clipping the wings of all dragons when they reach seven dragon years old, thus ensuring no dragon is able to fly. Grey is a very fit dragon, priding himself on good eating habits and exercise. He is however, very boring, has little conversational skills and sometimes a bumbler. |
| **Twin Lilac Dragons** | Brother and sister, the Lilac Twins are Draegonia's environmental engineers commonly known as the refuse disposal duo. They are always seen together with each one finishing the others sentence when they speak. They are the *'Jedward's' of Draegonia and even sport a similar head style. |
| **Dragon Indigo** | Indigo is a hard working young dragon holding down two jobs within the Hall of Dragons. He is both the security officer at night and during the day works in administrations. He is full of his own self importance. |

| | |
|---|---|
| **Flame Out** | The effect of a serious dragon illness or event. Should a dragon lose its flames, it most certainly, will slowly die. |
| **Dragon Time** | The Island of Draegonia is shrouded in a magical mist. All within the mist live their lives under Dragon Time where time outside the island's protective shield, almost stands still, in comparison. |
| **Garond** | An anagram of **Dragon.** |

*John Paul Henry Daniel Richard Grimes and Edward Peter Anthony Kevin Patrick Grimes (born 16 October 1991 in Dublin, Ireland) are an Irish pop duo. They are identical twins and perform under the name Jedward. Widely known for their blond quiffs, the twins first appeared as John & Edward on the sixth series of the UK TV show, The X Factor in 2009